ANCESTRAL VIRGINS

PART TWO

FIONA J. MACKINTOSH

MIDATLANTIC PRESS

CONTENTS

ANCESTRAL VIRGINS
Part Two

First published in the United States in 2026 by Midatlantic Press

Cover design by Florence Clementine
Cover image: Dame Gladys Cooper by Bassano Ltd, 1910
Photographs Collection, National Portrait Gallery, London, NPG x127674
Image colorization: micha_colors_pictures (Instagram)
Layout by Britta Jensen

Library of Congress Control Number: 2025922275
Publisher's Cataloging-in-Publication Data
provided by Five Rainbows Cataloging Services
Names: Mackintosh, Fiona J., 1957- author.
Title: Ancestral Virgins / Fiona J. Mackintosh.
Description: First edition. | Silver Spring, MD: Fiona J. Mackintosh, 2026. | Series: Albion's Millennium, bk. 1. | Also available in audiobook format.
Identifiers: ISBN 979-8-9934823-0-9 (paperback: vol. 1) | ISBN 979-8-9934823-1-6 (paperback: vol. 2) | ISBN 979-8-9934823-2-3 (paperback: vol. 3) | ISBN 979-8-9934823-3-0 (ebook: vol. 1) | ISBN 979-8-9934823-4-7 (ebook: vol. 2) | ISBN 979-8-9934823-5-4 (ebook: vol. 3)
Subjects: LCSH: Siblings--Fiction. | Young women--Fiction. | Family secrets--Fiction. | Down syndrome--Fiction. | Historical fiction. | World War, 1914-1918--Fiction. | BISAC: FICTION / Historical / 20th Century / World War I. | FICTION / World Literature / England / 20th Century. | FICTION / Literary. | GSAFD: Bildungsromans.
Classification: LCC full call number PS3508.M23 A53 2026 (print) | LCC PS3508.M23 (ebook) | DDC 813/.6--dc23.

Author's Note

Trigger warning: Readers should be aware that Part Two of *Ancestral Virgins* features violence associated with World War I.

Also, as I have never personally known anyone with Down's syndrome, I wanted to be sure that I had depicted the character of Davey Hallam accurately and with respect in the context of the historical period. Therefore, I'm grateful to Athena Pajer who drew on her own family experience in reading Davey's story with a keen and sensitive eye.

Chapter 10

September 1915

Captain Theodore "Tuggers" Crowindale of No. 11 Platoon, C Company of the 1st Nottinghamshire Infantry Regiment was dreaming about riding to hounds. He felt the rise and fall of a pure-bred hunter at full gallop between his hands and knees, the wind was on his face, and a blur of green flashed at the corner of his eyes.

A hand shook his shoulder. "You awake, Captain?"

Tuggers sat bolt upright, the horse beneath him gone. "Godolphin?"

"No, sir. Ramsbottom, sir."

Not his groom at Allenbury, but his batman, seventeen years old, from a mining village near Mansfield. "It's time, sir. There's light in the sky."

He struggled to his feet from the hay rick and brushed the straw from his greatcoat sleeves. His legs felt shaky as if he had been thrown roughly onto hard ground. The smell of the hunt remained, damp coverts, moss, and piles of wet leaves decaying. Beneath the great tall trees across the corner of the field, it was still very black, but a line of watery blue-grey light was easing its way upwards from the horizon.

To the north, up the line, there was the usual fireworks display, the crump and flare of shells bursting. The ground shook with each explosion, and sparks from the rockets spat in arcs across the still-dark sky. The rising mist was edged with the scent of cordite.

As the hunting field faded, the pit of Tuggers' stomach began its usual slow burn. For once, his sleep had taken him back to Allenbury. For once he'd not had one of his dreams – *Charlie Rockingham's eyeballs bursting and splattering him in the face.*

"Shall I fry up, sir? I got a couple of eggs from the farmer's wife last night."

"God no, not till after..."

"Yes, sir."

The bile rose to his throat at the thought of fat sizzling and spitting in the dixie lid.

"Just tea."

"Right away, sir."

The boy's face was so fresh under the tin helmet, tipped back, the strap marking the baby fat of his neck. Tuggers had to turn away from the perfection of the skin, that delicate membrane. It wasn't a fair fight, a boy's soft face against a slice of razor-sharp shrapnel.

Beyond the barn on the other side of the field, Tuggers could see the dark shape of his sergeant rousing the mound of greatcoats that were the sleeping soldiers of the detail. He'd asked his sergeant to choose the men for the job. The rest of the company were in their billets in Grenay, a mile inland from the lines.

Tuggers tamped down the tobacco in his pipe with his thumb and struck a match against the wall of the barn. He kept his matches in an old silver card case to keep them dry. It was the most useful thing he'd brought from home. He doubted that his mother would miss it. There wasn't much visiting for her to do at Allenbury anymore. He dragged the pipe smoke deep into his lungs. It stung, that first inhalation of the day, but by the third or fourth drag, he could no longer taste the sourness of his own mouth. He longed to clean his teeth, but toothbrushes were one of those luxuries reserved for life well behind the lines. As was washing. Other men seemed inured to living in their clothes for weeks, but he could never get used to it, the dirt in his nails, his ears, the corners of his eyes, the creases of his eyelids. The constant itching from the lice in the seams of his puttees and shirt. But it was the smell of himself he couldn't bear, the smell of rot, like the inside of his head was moulding away. He closed his eyes as he puffed on his pipe and let himself remember his valet shaving him with an open razor, the clean, soapy smell of the lather, the perfumed water, the warm towel on his face.

"Tea, sir."

He took the tin cup gingerly by its edge, the heat singeing the pads of his fingers and thumb. The condensed milk congealed on the surface of the tea like yellow turds. He put the mug down on a fence post and shouted for his sergeant, who came striding across the field as light started to spread across the eastern sky.

"Yes, Captain?"

"Sergeant, do you have someone watching the man's brother?" He was determined to prevent the brother from seeing what was to come. It was the least he could do.

"Two men, sir. He tried to fight them both so they had to take him down to Grenay and lock him up in the clink."

"Poor chap. It's terrible to think what he must be feeling."

"Yes, sir. Sad day, sir."

Sergeant Pilkington's face was impassive, but he averted his eyes.

Feeling his way over the hardened cart ruts, Tuggers led Pilkington around the barn to the field beyond the farmhouse. Two soldiers were shovelling earth around the base of a post from the farmer's wife's washing line. Tuggers came up close and fingered the hooks that had been screwed in the wood to secure the ropes. "This one's a little loose, Private. Make it secure."

"Yes, sir."

He heard an edge of sullenness in the young man's voice, and he felt compelled to speak. "Private, this is a black day for all of us."

"Yes, sir."

The same surly tone. It was hard to be the enemy in the men's eyes, hard to feel that he was losing their trust, the absolute trust they had shown him each time they had followed him up the line and over the top. He knew so much about each of them from censoring their decent, uncomplaining letters home.

Tuggers began pacing out the distance to the firing line, with Sergeant Pilkington in step beside him. "You mustn't mind them, sir. They know you did your best."

"Did I? Maybe there was something else I could have done. Maybe there still is..."

Even in the half-light, Tuggers could see in Pilkington's face that he was grasping at straws. After an awkward pause while Tuggers relit his pipe, the Sergeant ventured an opinion. "The lad did do a runner, sir. The Army can't be having that."

He was right. There was no getting away from it – Private Hallam had funked. He had disappeared from the company the day after the retreat from Loos. Tuggers had ordered a search, and he was soon found, hiding in an abandoned mine tower, the kind the French called *fosses*. Some deserters argued the hind legs off a donkey – they'd been carrying dispatches behind the line, they'd got lost, they'd been making their way back to the regiment – but this one just wailed and wept as the MPs dragged him out of the *fosse*.

When he was brought before Tuggers at the farmhouse billet some hours later, Hallam was still distraught, crying and making noises that might have been somebody's name. He slumped in a chair opposite Tuggers like a puppet whose strings had been cut. His teeth were chattering, saliva leaking from the sides of his mouth, and a nerve pulsed visibly in his cheek. It was his eyes that convinced Tuggers that he was mad, his staring eyes, the skin around them an unnatural papery-brown.

It wasn't possible to say "Come on, Private Hallam, do buck up" as he had planned. The words stuck in his throat. The man was beyond fear, he was in hell. His reason had fled, his spirit was destroyed, yet when Tuggers asked him his name and number, the boy rapped it out like clockwork, the first coherent words he had spoken since being found.

Tuggers knew it could just as easily have been him who cracked. How much horror could a man see before his mind broke from its hinges? Every time he woke sweating from another dream of Charlie Rockingham lying in No Man's Land just beyond reach of rescue for days – *eyeballs gone, giant rats scavenging in the chest cavity, dragging his guts through the mud* – he'd wonder if his mind would survive, even if his body by some fluke of fortune stayed alive. How many severed heads of men he knew, how many guts spilling from men in purple coils, how many of his friends burst apart by shells, sliced raw by shrapnel, heads pierced by bullets?

After a hasty court-martial in the bombed-out town hall in Grenay, after the boy was found guilty of desertion and condemned to death at dawn the next morning, Tuggers had appealed to Colonel Fitzwarren, the Battalion Commander, for clemency. "The man's nerves are shattered, sir. He's not faking it. I've never seen a worse case."

"Sorry, old chap, but a funk is a funk. He may be the genuine article, but imagine what ideas it would give the other chaps if we sent him to a rest home with a pat on the back. Can't be soft on deserters, Captain, you know that. Nobody likes these occasions, but it's jolly well got to be done."

Sergeant Pilkington cleared his throat. "Sir, it's time to get the prisoner. The sun is coming up."

There was no escaping it now, the wheels were in motion. Tuggers walked with Pilkington to the door of the farmhouse, ducking his head to avoid the low lintel beam. The kitchen was hot after the mild outdoor air, steam rising from a pot on the fire. Tuggers nodded to the farmer lacing his boots in a chair by the window. The farmer's wife spoke in rapid French, "*Soyez gentille avec ce jeune homme en haut, Monsieur, je vous en pris.*"

How many times was he to take the blame for a terrible decision he had opposed? He pressed the woman's hand, feeling the roughness of her palm against his own. *"C'est pas possible, Madame, je suis desolé."*

She pulled her hand from his and turned away, poking the fire till the sparks flew up the chimney. The sweat rose in the small of his back. He let Sergeant Pilkington lead the way up the steep stairs. It was much colder upstairs. A young soldier who had been sitting on the floor outside the locked door scrambled to his feet and saluted. Sergeant Pilkington rapped on the door. "Company Commander Crowindale here to see the prisoner."

The young soldier turned the key, and Sergeant Pilkington pushed open the door and stood aside to let Tuggers enter first. An officer in a dog collar jumped to his feet as Tuggers entered.

"At ease, Padre."

The man sat back down abruptly into his chair as if his legs were too weak to hold him upright. The only light in the room came from the uncurtained window, though there was a drift of smoke as if a candle had just been snuffed out. Tuggers could just make out the prisoner curled in a ball on the bed, his back to the room. "How's he been, Padre?"

The young chaplain cleared his throat and then coughed into his fist. "He's been like this most of the time, Captain. Maybe asleep, but I'm not sure. Some moaning and groaning and, once, he shouted like the hounds of hell were after him. I prayed all night for his soul, but he didn't seem to hear me."

Even in the half-light, Tuggers could see the chaplain's pallor. "Sergeant, give the Padre a nip. He's earned it."

Sergeant Pilkington opened his greatcoat. From a low inside pocket, he pulled out a flask of Scotch. He unscrewed the top and handed it to the chaplain. "I'm afraid it's a question of swigging it straight, sir."

The chaplain nodded, took a long swallow and handed it back. "Thanks, Captain. Decent of you."

"We'll see you down at the field in a few moments, Padre."

The chaplain stood up again, steadied himself and then moved quickly out of the room and down the stairs.

Tuggers nodded to Sergeant Pilkington. The Sergeant hesitated and then handed Tuggers the flask before leaving the room. As the door closed behind him, Tuggers stood for a minute, trying to hear the boy's breathing over the distant boom of the fighting, but everything in the room was completely still. When he spoke, he could almost see the words unfurl in the chilly air in front of him like a banner. "Private Hallam, I am here to take you to your place of punishment. It's time."

There was no movement from the boy's body. Tuggers felt a surge of hope. Perhaps the boy had died of fright in the night. Perhaps the whole repugnant spectacle could now be aborted. He saw himself coming out of the farmhouse as the sun rose above the hedgerows and striding across the field towards the firing squad, seeing the relief on their faces when he stood them down.

And then the young man turned over on the bed. "Captain?"

Tuggers came closer to the bed. "Yes, Len?"

The boy sat up slowly and swung his legs over the side of the bed, feeling around him with his hands like a blind man. "Sir?"

Tuggers sat down next to him. "I'm here, Len. Here, take a drink of this. It'll help."

The boy took the flask and tried to raise it to his mouth, but his hands were shaking too violently. Tuggers reached over and steadied it for him while he drank, and Tuggers saw his own hand was trembling too. "Len, I'm sorry to say the time has come."

"Captain Crowindale, sir?"

"Yes, Len."

"I'm very sorry for the trouble I've caused you, sir. You've been good to me..."

"Come along, man, no need for that."

"I'm better off dead, I know that now. I'm no use to anyone the way I am."

"Nonsense, man. You're ill, that's all. You aren't to blame."

The boy's head fell forward, as if he couldn't bear the weight of it. "My mother, she'll be so ashamed."

"Nonsense, Private. You mustn't say that. You've served your country well."

Tuggers felt the hollowness of the words even as he spoke them.

"No sir, I haven't, but never mind that now."

He reached into the inside pocket of his greatcoat and pulled out his paybook. Opening the waterproof cover, he pulled out a letter and handed it to Tuggers. "Please will you make sure she gets this?"

"I will."

Tuggers laid it carefully inside his own paybook. He put his hand under the boy's arm and helped him up. The boy's tremor made it hard to stand so Tuggers held his arm, and together they moved towards the door.

"Sergeant!" Tuggers called.

The door opened, and Sergeant Pilkington stepped in.

"Len, I'm afraid we must tie your hands and shackle your legs."

The boy nodded mutely, turning his head away as the young soldier who had been guarding the door helped Sergeant Pilkington to tie the ropes around his wrists and ankles. Tuggers led the way down the stairs, hearing the shackled boy take one step at a time. As they emerged into the steamy kitchen, the farmer's wife turned away and put her head in her apron, and the farmer, his hands in his pockets, nodded emphatically at no one in particular.

Outside, most of the sky was light, though the sun hadn't yet risen above the hedgerows. Tuggers breathed in the smell of wet earth and wood smoke in the mild air and allowed himself to be thankful that he would live through this day. Often enough, knee-deep in trench mud or poised on the firestep as bullets singed his ears, he had not been able to tell himself as much. Watching Len Hallam stumble along between Sergeant Pilkington and the guard, Tuggers felt the agony the boy must feel knowing that these were the last steps he would ever take through dew-soaked grass, the last time he would feel the air on his skin, the warmth of the just dawning sun on his face.

Across the field, the firing post stood up against the watery blue sky. Pigeons cooed in the quiet between the distant booms of the big guns. Now it was light, Tuggers could see the hips and haws and holly berries dotting the brambled tangles of the hedgerow just as they would be at Allenbury. It would almost be cubbing season, back in the days when he had no greater worry on his mind than choosing between a dull debate in the Lords or staying up for the Wednesday hunt.

From the direction of Grenay, Colonel Fitzwarren came trotting up into the field on his big grey mare. As Sergeant Pilkington and the guard turned Len around and backed him up to the post, wrapping ropes around his torso, the slow roll of drums began, and six young men with rifles on their shoulders began their short march from the barn to the firing line, boys who had joined up with Len Hallam from the farm estates and pit villages of Nottinghamshire and had fought with them through the carnage of the last year. On Tuggers' instructions, Sergeant Pilkington had loaded the Enfields himself, five with live ammunition and one with a blank round so each soldier would know he might not have fired the shot that killed his comrade. It was a fine tradition, but whoever fired the blank round would know as his rifle wouldn't kick.

The soldiers wheeled about and came to attention. Colonel Fitzwarren nodded to Tuggers, who walked across to the post and stood beside Len as the chaplain said a prayer in a shaky voice that sounded muffled in the open air.

"Yea though I walk through the valley of the shadow of death, I will fear no evil, for thou art with me, thy rod and thy staff, they comfort me. Dear Lord, receive the soul of this man, your servant, unto your care and forgive him his trespasses. Amen."

The chaplain made a quick motion of benediction over Len's

head and hurried away. Tuggers stepped forward and pinned a white patch on the chest of the boy's tunic over his heart as if he were pinning on a medal. The boy sagged against him, weeping, his face against Tuggers' shoulder.

"I'm frightened, sir, I'm so afraid."

"Steady on, old man. Try to be strong."

Desperately Tuggers tried to remember a phrase from the King James Bible, any snatch that might console, but nothing would come. Nothing but the Christ on the Cross crying out "Why have you forsaken me?"

The boy wept now, his voice rising to shrill keening. "Please, please don't let them do it, sir, please don't let them..."

This was beyond bearing. Tuggers pushed Len off his shoulder and, in one swift movement, threw the terrible sackcloth hood over the boy's head and tightened the drawstring. He hurried away across the field, fighting the nausea that he could feel at the back of his throat. Standing apart from Sergeant Pilkington and the medical officer, he drew his loaded revolver as the Colonel had ordered. The Colonel's horse sidled and jibbed, and, holding the reins in one hand, the Colonel turned it back to face the action. In his other hand, he held up a handkerchief. For an instant it hung there, flaring in the light from the rising sun, and then with a flourish, he brought down his arm.

A volley of shots rang out, and pigeons burst wildly out of the stubble. Len slumped forward against the ropes, blood spurting from his arm and chest. The firing squad turned away, and one man bent over and vomited. Every muscle in Tuggers' body went slack with relief, and he felt a sudden rush in his bowels. It was over.

The medical officer hurried over and felt the boy's pulse, but, turning towards the Colonel, shook his head urgently. It could not be. The boy wasn't dead. Colonel Fitzwarren looked over to where Tuggers stood rooted to the spot, horrified, his hand slack on his pistol.

"Captain Crowindale, if you please."

Tuggers had shot his beloved old and infirm hunting dog in the past, and even a thoroughbred with a broken leg. He knew it was an act of love. And in the heat of combat, he had shot Germans in any part of their bodies he could aim at, even their faces. But he had never shot a fellow man in cold blood. Which was what he was being ordered to do now.

Cocking his revolver, Tuggers walked towards the post, aware of every eye on his back. He felt the ropes chafe against the skin of his own wrists, the heat of his own terrified breath inside the suffocating hood. As he drew close, he saw the blood pooling and spreading in a dark stain through the grass and thought for a second that the boy was already dead, but the hooded head lifted, as if the boy could see him approaching, and a sound came from within the hood, a sound that was barely human, and Tuggers put his revolver to the creature's head and pulled the trigger.

Lying on his cot in the upstairs bedroom of an abandoned merchant's house in Grenay, Tuggers tried to write the letter to the boy's family. In the light of an oil lamp, he'd peeled off his mud-encrusted uniform and washed himself with a billy can of hot water Ramsbottom had boiled up and a tiny sliver of soap he kept wrapped in paper at the bottom of his kitbag. But the dirt lingered in the crevasses of his body, especially in his blistered feet. He'd sent Ramsbottom down to the kitchen to wash his filthy pairs of socks and stuffed his boots with straw to draw out the moisture from two weeks in the trenches.

Lying on the cot, Tuggers propped his ruined feet on the low windowsill. The evening air felt chill but soothing on his soles. In the next room, three subalterns laughed and shouted as they drank and played cards. Outside, soldiers clattered down the cobbled street heading toward the *estaminet*. From where he lay, Tuggers saw a line of poplars silhouetted against arcs and sprays of gold, red, and white from the front.

The echo of his days-old beard still itched even after he'd shaved it off. Images flared and roiled in his head – the blood-soaked limber, the dead man's arm hanging off the side and banging against the gatepost, the trussed-up corpse slithering into the shallow grave, the makeshift cross with his name written in burnt cork. *Charlie's collapsed face turning green, then grey, then a slick of black slime.*

Tuggers sat up abruptly and read over what he had written.

Dear Mrs. Hallam,

I'm sorry to have to inform you that your son, Private Len Hallam of the 1ˢᵗ Nottinghamshire, was killed in action this morning in the Loos sector. In the manner of his death, he showed great courage, and you would be proud of how he gave his life for his country.

A knock on the door, and Sergeant Pilkington came in.

"Did you get some dinner, Sergeant?"

"Yes, sir. A splendid dinner, thank you. Made a nice change from ration biscuits and bully beef."

"Well, don't get used to it. I reckon we'll be back up the line in a few days."

"Right-o, sir."

Tuggers scrawled his signature on the letter in front of him and folded it. "Here's the notification letter. Can you seal it and make sure it goes off as soon as possible? I've been vague with his mother about how he died – there's no need to tell her the details. And I'll arrange to have Private Hallam put on the Died on Active Service register, that way his mother'll get a pension."

Sergeant Pilkington's face looked pained.

"Is there a problem with that, Sergeant?"

"It's too late, sir, I'm sorry to say. I heard the RSM saying that they've already wired home with the news."

"What did the telegram say?"

"Dunno, sir, but I imagine it mentioned his court-martial and whatnot."

The Sergeant's delicacy in not calling a spade a spade was not lost on Tuggers. He turned and looked out of the window towards the cartwheels of light in the sky beyond the poplars. He looked back at the Sergeant. "Bring the brother to me. Is he still in the clink?"

"No, sir. Remember, you ordered me to release him? But I think the MPs are keeping an eye on him – they'll know where he is. Back in a jiffy."

Tuggers lay back down on his cot and closed his eyes. He held his breath deeply in his lungs and then exhaled. He wondered how much longer he would be able to draw a simple breath. In the lulls between shelling, he heard the leaves of the poplars rustling and the swift hoot of an owl. Again, he held a deep, full breath and then released it. He tried to imagine he was a peace-time traveller, relaxing in a French inn after a long day of tramping through unspoiled country lanes, his stomach full of fresh trout, crusty bread, a runny Camembert set off by the tart local red wine. And then he heard the thud of boots climbing the wooden stairs of the house, and he swung his legs off the cot and stood up.

There was a knock on the door.

"Enter!"

Sergeant Pilkington came in with his hand on the shoulder of a young soldier with shiny dark hair swept back off a high forehead. The boy gave a cursory salute.

"At ease, Private Hallam. Sergeant, you may leave us."

Tuggers saw Pilkington was reluctant to go. He gave a nod towards the door and, as the door closed behind the Sergeant, Tuggers was alone with the dead man's brother. He was suddenly aware of the chill of the floorboards on the soles of his feet.

He pulled out a wooden chair from against the wall. "Sit down, Tom."

The boy remained standing. His gaze was fixed on a point far beyond Tuggers' shoulder.

"Tom, I'm ordering you to sit down."

Still, he stood, and Tuggers stood too, watching and waiting. There was a loud explosion somewhere beyond the village. Both men ducked to look out of the low window under the eaves. Orange flames lit up the indigo sky like a sudden violent dawn.

"Ammunition dump," Tuggers said, turning away from the window. How many men were dying right now in that blaze, their skin turning black and peeling off their bones.

Barely perceptibly the boy nodded, then sat down abruptly on the chair. Tuggers sank back onto his cot, looked down at his hands and swallowed. "I'm very sorry about what happened to your brother, Tom. I want you to know I asked the CO to invalid him back home, but Battalion Command wouldn't hear of it. He was ill – we know that, you and I, but I'm afraid the Army takes a dim view of desertion, whatever the reasons."

The boy stood up. "Will that be all, sir?"

Startled, Tuggers looked up the long, lean length of the boy's body and tried to be angry. He should put the boy on dirty jobs or have him tied to a limber wheel for insubordination. But then he saw the boy's face. It was folded in on itself, trying to hold it all in, behind a desperate, dogged frown, yet in the cheek a nerve pulsed.

Tuggers stood up. "Go home, Tom."

The boy's eyes flew to Tuggers' face. "Pardon, sir?"

"I said go home. I'll have Sergeant Pilkington prepare your papers for a week of compassionate leave. Go home and be with your mother."

A spasm passed over the boy's face. "Thank you, sir."

"Dismissed, Private Hallam."

The boy saluted and moved towards the door.

"Wait."

The boy looked back. Tuggers' tunic hung over the bedpost, and he fumbled in the pockets and pulled Len's letter out of his paybook, a little crushed at the corners. "Give your mother this. But make sure she's had the news first, old man, all right?"

In the first hours after the execution, he'd opened the letter to censor it but couldn't bring himself to cut out any of the boy's last words. Tom took the letter, staring at the quavery handwriting on the flap.

"And don't come back."

The words were out of Tuggers' mouth before he knew it. Confusion clouded the boy's eyes. They looked at each other as Tuggers wrestled with how to make his meaning clear. "Find a way. Your mother has suffered enough."

The boy stood motionless, still staring at Tuggers, holding the letter stiffly away from him. And then his eyes cleared.

Tuggers nodded towards the door. "Go."

The boy turned and left, his boots loud on the stairs. From the window, Tuggers watched him walk a few steps in the street then break into a sprint, arms pumping by his sides. If Sergeant Pilkington had listened at the door, Tuggers might yet face his own court-martial. It was all he could do, and yet it was almost nothing. He lay back down on the cot, hands above his head, surrendered and dog tired, but as his eyelids closed, the monstrous blood-caked hood rose like a terrible snake, jerking and twitching. Tuggers leapt up and pushed the window open wider with quaking hands, fighting to draw air into his lungs. Above the town, the clouds hung bloated and ruddy as the ammunition dump continued to burn.

CHAPTER 11

AUGUST 11, 1911

When the coal-black horses tossed their heads to shake off the flies, the great black plumes dipped and waved like palm trees in the Bible. May Hallam had never seen anything as elegant in the whole world as those feathers. She longed to touch one, run her hands along the softness, feel the grain of it, over and over, smoothing and touching, but they were too high. Instead, she reached up to press her finger to the plump and shiny heart of the nearest rosette on the dray, but Mam snatched her hand back and held it in hers.

It was then the bells began. Not like they rang on Sundays, cheerfully, and not like the peals that spilled like a waterfall over couples who'd just been married, coming out from the church into the sunlight, the bride lifting her posy to shield her eyes. It was like a hammer hitting a rock, slow and hard and terrible.

May's back itched in her new clothes. Out of the corner of her eye, she saw her brother Tom, the eldest of them all, holding Mam's arm like a policeman stopping someone from running away. High in the yews, the usual summer birds chattered and trilled even as the bell tolled. At the lychgate, the undertaker's men in their top hats with the long streamers slid the long eerie box off the dray and lifted it up onto their shoulders. May looked back to see if Davey had noticed this feat of strength, but he was looking up at the sky, turning back and forth on his heels as he held Aunt Emma's hand.

The hot air pressed against her like rabbit fur. She breathed it in, feeling it warm on the insides of her nostrils and the insides of her eyelids. There was no escape from the clutch of it. In the winter you could wear two pairs of socks inside your boots, wrap yourself in a horse blanket and crouch by the fire. Or run up and down the hill to Granny Maitland's to get your blood up and your limbs loose and warm. All there was in summer was the pond, skittered with duckweed and yellowing teazles.

Inside, the church was a cool, dark cave. They walked behind the box, she and Mam and Tom in front. She was surprised to be ushered into a pew near the front where the gentry usually sat. She could see the notches in the pillar left by horsemen riding off to the Crusades. Every Sunday after service, her father used to lift her and Davey up to run their fingers over the slits in the stone.

The undertaker's men settled the box on a trestle at the altar. Beside her, Mam held a handkerchief across her mouth, but no sounds came out. A patch of sweat darkened the armpit of her new black blouse. On the other side of Mam sat Tom and Len, one dark, one lighter, both with scaly skin and Adam's apples that stuck out of their long, skinny necks. Then Lily and Ada, their hair tamped with brushing and water, in their new black dresses bought with the insurance, everything made too large to leave room for growing. And, next to Aunt Emma, Davey, his head shaped like a jack-o'-lantern, narrower at the temples than the chin, and eyes narrow as a Chinaman's. His head was tipped back looking up at the dusty church rafters, blinking in his usual way. Her own Davey.

In the pulpit, the Vicar was talking about God, and sometimes May heard her father's name.

"Cyril Hallam was a good man..." "...the best kind of yeoman, a true Englishman in his service to his betters..." "No one knew horses like Cyril Hallam..."

Suddenly May was running her nails along the ridges of her father's corduroy britches to dislodge the caked dust and mud and smelling the grainy old seed bag he wore as an apron. He'd smelled of tobacco and horse sweat when she rode beside him on the driver's seat of the trap when he went to Burton Joyce to look at a workhorse for sale. He'd let her hold the pony's head as he went into the field to examine the Shire, but she'd had to call out for him when the pony set off down the lane, her hands clamped to its bridle, her feet dragging in the dust.

"Cyril Hallam was a man who put his devotion to duty before all other things..."

She remembered sitting with Davey at the kitchen table cutting up the newspaper to make paper dolls, helping him as he tried to work the scissors – "That's it, put your thumb through the top hole and press down" – and looking up, she saw Dada in his chair put his hand up to cover his wet eyes.

After the service ended with a slow sad hymn, they all stood in silence as the strong men lifted the box onto their shoulders. With a little push on May's shoulders, Mam urged her to budge down the pew and follow the men down the aisle. Together they walked behind the box from the dreary indoors out into the blazing sunlight and along the path round the side of the church.

In the shade of the yews, the men lowered the box on straps into a hole in the ground. May stood at the edge, a ball of grass and dirt in her hand. She saw how the earth had been sliced cleanly open like bread and thought of the caterpillars and earthworms and how their darkness must suddenly have been cleaved open, and her mother had to take the dirt from her hand and drop it herself. It landed with a thud on the lid of the box, like a snowball thrown at an outhouse door.

At the cottage, Mrs. Coulter from next door had the kettle boiling and the front door propped open to the yard to let in what little air there was. May rested her chin on the kitchen table and breathed in the good smells of paste sandwiches, hard-boiled eggs, and fresh-baked scones. Gooseberry and rhubarb pies sat on the window ledge to cool. There was Dada's homemade wine, cloudy and mysterious in its stoppered bottles, and Mam sent Tom down to the pub for jugs of beer.

Mam put a clean apron on over her blacks and helped Mrs. Coulter and Mrs. Miller pour the teas. The men stood in the doorway, talking in low voices, looking too large for the indoor space and hot in their Sunday suits. Their red hands hung by their sides except when they took out their large handkerchiefs and mopped their faces.

May ducked between their legs and stepped down into the dim light of the parlour. It looked different full of people. Aunt Emma sat with the Vicar and Mrs. Walton, the schoolmistress, telling them one of her long stories, stroking Ada's arm absently as she talked. The heavy curtains were drawn to shut out the sun. A large framed photograph of Dada leaned against the cushions of the settle as Mam had had no time to hang it before the service. Dada's face, his eyeballs strangely white, seemed to hover in the shadowy parlour. No one sat beside it, and he seemed lonely there by himself so May climbed up onto the slippery silk and leaned her head against the hard edge of the frame.

"Mam!" Ada shouted, "Look at May. See what she's doing."

May froze. Mam put her head around the door, her eyes weary.

"What is it, Ada?"

"It's May. The silly clot's playing with Dada's picture."

She hadn't known not to touch the picture. Her mother moved into the room, and May shut her eyes, but at the sound of a slap, her eyes flew open and saw Ada nursing her arm.

"Leave her be," Mam said. "She's only five for goodness sake. She's doing it no harm."

Avoiding Ada's look, May slid off the settle and ducked through the legs and out into the yard where hens pecked hopefully at the dirt. The heat was a muddling blaze. From beyond the hedge on the embankment came the drowsy hum of Granny Maitland's bees, and, through the slits of her eyes, she saw Davey in his new black trousers, sitting on the ground hacking at it with a teaspoon. Weaving through the hens, May squatted beside him. He held out the spoon, and she slid it into a crack and pressed down hard on the handle, feeling it bend in her fingers.

"Aunt Emma's going to adopt you now Dada's dead."

It always sounded like Davey had cotton wool in his mouth, but May never missed a word. She shook her head. "No, she isn't. Mam said she wouldn't hear of it." She'd listened at the door and had forgotten Davey had been with her. Afterwards, Mam had told her Aunt Emma had meant to be kind and was lonely in that big house now Uncle Roy was gone, but Mam said she couldn't do without her.

"Yes, but if you'd been adopted, would you have run away?"

She looked across the yard through the haze of thistledown and tiny insects. Even the thought of leaving them all was making her stomach hurt. This was her place, this yard, this square of dirt and dust. She pressed harder on the spoon. "I'm not going to be adopted, Davey, I told you."

There was the rattle of a dogcart pulling up beyond the hedge. They scrambled up and ran to the gate where the estate manager was climbing down from the cart, the reins in his hand. He was wearing his usual tweed suit but had a black armband on his sleeve.

"Is that on account of our dad dying, Mr. Kilkenny?" May asked, her chin resting on the gate.

"Aye, it is." Mr. Kilkenny hooked the reins over the gatepost. "So, are you bairns going to let me by or am I going to have to vault?"

May pulled Davey to one side. "Mam's in the house with all the people."

He came through and carefully latched the gate behind him. The children were so close to his legs that he took an uneasy step back. He reached out a hand and rumpled Davey's hair. Then he looked beyond Davey to May.

"Gie the pony a drop of water, would you? Here's a penny for you and your brother."

May made Davey hold the bucket while she pumped, but he wouldn't hold it still so they both got water on their boots. Leaving the pony to drink, they crept indoors. A lot of people were crowded into the parlour. May wedged Davey into a space near the piano and crouched beside him, feeling his wet-lipped breath on her face. Mr. Kilkenny sat on the settle next to Dada's picture, holding a delicate teacup in his large hand.

"Mrs. Hallam, his Lordship sends his condolences and deep regrets for no' being able to come, but he was obliged to stay in London for the emergency debate."

Aunt Emma leaned forward and nudged Mam's arm with the back of her hand. "To think that he even thought of coming. What an honour, Addie."

Mam bowed her head to Mr. Kilkenny but said nothing.

"Forgive me for mentioning business on this sad day, but I thought it would put your mind at rest to know that his Lordship is verra willing for you to stay on in this house given that your sons will still be working for us up at the stables."

Again, Mam nodded. "They're good boys. Hard workers."

"I'm well aware of that, Mrs. Hallam. Your husband was the best waggoner Mummersford's ever had, and I'm sure he led by his example in his household."

Mam sat very still but looked like she'd swallowed something large and hard with sharp edges. Aunt Emma glanced at her. "Of course, Addie would've liked the boys to try for grammar school, but seeing how things stand, she knows they're better off working for the estate. His Lordship'll see them right, I'm sure."

Mam beckoned to May who jumped up and went to her side. "Go and find Tom and Len and tell them to come and thank Mr. Kilkenny. And tell them to be quick."

"Where are they?"

"I don't know. Outside somewhere I should think. No, Davey, you stay here with me."

Outside, the shadows were stretching out across the wheat fields. The men smoking their pipes out in the lane pointed down the road towards the pond when she asked for her brothers. She found Tom and Len standing side by side on the bank, throwing stones at the ducks. She slid down the bank towards them, feeling pond water seep into her boots.

"Mam says you've to go home and thank Mr. Kilkenny."

Tom pulled his arm back and let loose a stone that flew far across the pond, and a scatter of ducks flew up squawking. "What d'you mean, thank him?"

"What I said. Mam's waiting."

Dragonflies zipped and zapped across the pond like tiny slivers of sky. The boys looked at each other, dark-eyed Tom with the frown lines between his eyes, Len with his mild face and long scarecrow limbs, and May thought she saw their shoulders sag. She stood beside them, ankle-deep in the water, watching the overlapping circles rippling out across the pond as fish after fish broke the surface. May plunged her hand into the water and closed her fingers around a flint. "Here's a good one, Len."

She held it out to him, but he hesitated. "What about Mam?"

May lifted her face to a hint of an evening breeze from out of the west. "Mam's all right. Are you going to throw that stone or can I have a go?"

The moon was caught like a fish in the gap between the cotton curtains, its silver tail lying across the bed. A fox barked somewhere out in the copses, and May hoped she'd remembered to latch the door of the henhouse. There were still adult voices downstairs in the kitchen where moths would be looping around the lamp. Aunt Emma had left with the estate manager, who'd offered to drive her to the railway station – "Well, if you're quite sure it's not out of your way, Mr. Kilkenny" – but others had stopped on, some from the village and even one or two from the estate. Mam hadn't come up as she usually did to see that the girls brushed their hair and hung their clothes up in the press. She'd wished them goodnight downstairs and turned back to the conversation, a mug of beer in front of her on the kitchen table.

A drift of smoke from the candle still hung in the room. Through the open window, May breathed in lavender and the sharpness of rosemary and the winey smell of apples rotting in the grass. A sharp feather pricked her back, and she ran her hand over the bolster till she found it and pulled it out with her thumb and fingernail. Ada, in her sleep, moaned and turned over, wrapping the sheet around her. On the other side of Ada, Lily lay facing the wall. May watched the curve of her under the nightdress, looking for the even rise and fall of sleep, but then her ear caught a tiny, high-pitched noise that sounded far away.

"Lily?" she whispered. "What is it?"

Lily's shoulders rose slowly up towards her ears.

"Are you crying for Dada? He's in heaven now so it's all right, you know."

Lily sat up suddenly, her fine golden hair standing out from her head in an electric web. "It isn't!" she whispered fiercely.

"Why isn't it? The Vicar told us, he said he's in a better place."

A slow, deep snore rose from Ada, wrapped like a mummy in the sheet.

"Yes, but he's not *here*, don't you see?" Lily hissed, "He'll never be here again."

And now there was a great whirling in May's mind like bats. Nothing in this day had prepared her for never again, nothing in the excitement and bustle of the funeral and the kind looks people gave her in the street, the sense of importance and ceremony.

Her father had not been a part of it, but he'd simply stepped aside for a moment. He was up at the stables tending to a sick horse or had gone into town for the livestock sales. He would be back. How could he not be back? His pipe was still on the table by the fire. The smell of him was still everywhere in the house, a mixture of tobacco and horsehair and male sweat.

He couldn't just have vanished into nowhere. It made no sense at all. And yet, and yet, that word *never* was now tolling in May's mind like the church bell had tolled that morning. *Never, never, never.* So this was what dead meant, this violent wrenching away, this empty space where a person had stood just days or hours before. She curled her knees up to her chin and wrapped her arms around them, in the first true anguish of knowing her father was gone and would never come home again.

CHAPTER 12

JUNE 1914

There it was again – a muffled buzzing like a bee trapped in a jar and then nothing. May swung her legs out of bed and pulled on the woollen socks that lay like dead things on the floor. Through the wall came the snorts and murmurings of her three brothers deep in sleep, but otherwise silence. At the top of the stairs, she edged past the bucket under the place where the rain always came in and saw the lamp burning on the kitchen table and her mother's back bent over the sewing machine. May saw her foot press the pedal and realised the source of the buzzing. She slipped quietly down the stairs, but her mother's eyes were too sharp for her.

"It's not time to get up yet, Maysie."

May came up behind her and leaned against her mother's shoulder.

"Is that my costume?"

"No, it's Ada's. Yours and Davey's are on the chair."

She glanced over to where some folded clothes lay in a pile. Yawning, she leaned in closer to her mother.

"It's cold. Why d'you let the fire go out?"

"We're not made of wood, you know. But if you're stopping, make yourself useful and stir it back up."

May opened the range door and poked at the glowing ashes with a piece of kindling. She arranged two half logs propped against each other and pumped at the ashes with the bellows until the bark caught and began to crackle. Latching the range door closed, she dragged a kitchen chair close to the sewing machine and sat down, pulling her knees up to her chin to warm herself. Her mother turned the piece of blue material around and ran up a seam.

"That's the boys' old eiderdown."

"And now it's Britannia's cloak."

It was getting lighter in the room. A first bird began to stir and chatter in the hedge.

"Did you sleep at all, Mam?"

"I dozed for a while in the chair. Couldn't sleep for long with three pageant costumes to make."

"I'd have helped."

"Not on this machine you wouldn't. I don't want you sticking a needle through your fingernail."

May shuddered but couldn't stop herself from asking. "Did you ever do that?"

Her mother glanced sideways at her as she bit off a thread. "No, but my sister Winnie did once. She screamed like a stuck pig."

May was sorry she'd asked. She rested her cheek on her night-gowned knees. A log popped in the range. "Tell me again about how I got my name."

Her mother sat back in her chair, her hands resting in the satiny folds of the eiderdown. "Well, naming a child is always a big responsibility. Your father and I wanted you all to have names with significance, something we could tell you about as you grew. Tom and Len are named for your two grandfathers, Lily's after my mother, Ada after me of course, Davey after a brother of Dada's who died when he was very small. And then eight years ago when you came along, we were going to call you Ethel after Mother Hallam, but the day after you were born, I looked out the window at a sea of apple and hawthorn blossom, and I knew you had to be May. I wanted you to be reminded of that glorious sight all your long life."

"Will I live for a long time?"

"Of course you will. Now get that kettle on while I finish this."

May slid off the chair and, picking up the kettle with both hands, carried it into the scullery. By the deep stone sink, her brother's razors lay sheathed on a shelf too high for Davey to reach. As she pumped water into the kettle, she stared at the large cobweb dotted with flies that she wouldn't let anyone knock down. In a tin bucket, rags were soaking in blush pink water, meaning Mam must be on her monthlies again. She'd never entirely explained what they were, except to say it was a curse all women had to bear for the chance to have their children, but May shouldn't be afraid when her turn came.

May staggered back into the kitchen with the heavy kettle and, with a great heave, hoisted it up on top of the range. Through the window, it was light enough to see the hedge. The needle on the sewing machine was moving so fast that it seemed like Mam was barely able to feed the material into it fast enough. As she took her foot off the pedal, the machine whirred to a stop, and she pulled the material out and held it up in front of her. "Finished!"

The blue eiderdown was now edged with golden rickrack and had been hemmed and gathered at the top and threaded through with a curtain tie with a lush ball and fringe at each end.

Her mother put a cover over the sewing machine and tucked her workbasket underneath.

"Why do we have to be soldiers and Ada gets to be Britannia?"

Lifting the funnel from the lamp, Mam blew out the flame. "Never mind that now," she said, casting a glance to the ceiling. "Before the others are up, I need to tell you something."

May paused in the middle of spooning tea into the pot.

"I've decided. Once school is over for the summer, you're going to visit Lily."

May's mouth dropped open. "By myself?"

"Yes. Well, Mrs. Craddock will take you on the train – she's going to Brighton to visit her sister. And then Lily'll bring you back when she comes for her summer holiday. And in the meantime, she'll be able to show you what it's like to be in service – some tips and suchlike."

There was confusion in May's head, but one thought rose above all the others. "What about Davey?"

Her mother put her hands on May's shoulders. "That's why I'm doing it, Maysie. He needs to learn how to do without you for a bit."

"But he'll hate it."

"I know, but Ada and the rest of us will be here with him. He'll soon adjust, you'll see."

"But why not Ada? Can't she go instead?"

Her mother sighed and lifted her arms to tidy the hair that had escaped from her bun. With a pin between her teeth, she replied, "She can go next year. It's time Davey was apart from you, and I can't very well send *him* away, can I?"

May put the lid back on the tea caddy, pushing down on it hard to make sure it was tight. Suddenly all the ordinary things in the room seemed impossible to live without. She felt a surge of affection for the brown teapot with the chip in its spout, the fireguard, the rag rug, the row of upturned boots on the fender. What if these things made her who she was? What if without them she was nobody, with no substance or edges or even a voice that anyone could hear? Guilt, disbelief, and a wild sense of possibility were balls of air in her gut. "I'm going to the privy."

As the kettle began to whistle, there was the sound of feet hitting the floor upstairs.

"Off you go then – and be quick. The boys'll be out there any minute."

May shoved her feet into her unlaced boots and pulled a shawl off the peg rack. Outside it was warmer than she'd expected, and a fine misty rain hung in the air. She walked up the narrow path between the chicken coop and the potato patch, pausing to pick a raspberry from the canes, smooshing the fruit against the top of her mouth with her tongue for the pleasure of the juice. Standing on the mossy stone step, she reached up to unlatch the outhouse door, which creaked open, letting out the familiar smell of wood, earth, and rotten eggs. It was dusky inside with the door closed. She pulled up her nightgown and winced as her bottom touched the cold boards of the bench. A few loud bursts of air, and as her pee flew out of her, down, down, down into the deep stink of the pit, her stomach settled.

When she'd thrown the soiled bits of newspaper down the hole and closed the wooden lid, she came out, blinking at the bright silver curtain of cloud. On the higher ground behind the garden, Granny Maitland's bees hummed in the borage and comfrey. May felt another clutch of panic. What would happen if she went beyond the sound of those bees? Who would she be without them?

Down below in the yard, Tom was pumping water into a bucket, his shirt sleeves rolled to his elbows. Through the kitchen window, May saw her mother frying bacon at the range, Len cutting the loaf, Ada pouring the tea, and Davey, her own dear Davey, reaching across the table on his elbows for the jam pot. Was this how it would be once she was gone, the space where she used to be closed over and she already forgotten?

When the hands of the clock showed two o'clock, the children walked in pairs from the schoolhouse to the church hall, Davey's hand sweaty in hers. In the dusty room behind the stage, amidst all the children jostling and shouting, May helped Davey to put on his costume. He was delighted with the sackcloth tunic, smoothing down the nap of it over and over, but he baulked when she tried to lower the cardboard helmet over his large, round head. "I can't breathe."

"Yes, you can. Look, Mam made this nice big hole at the front so you can see everything and breathe the air and sing the songs."

"I don't like it."

"I know, but it's not for very long. And look, I'll have one on too, see?" She looked out at him from the fortress her head had become inside the cardboard, but she could still see doubt in his eyes. "Tell you what, if you wear the helmet, we can go up to Home Farm afterwards and see Tom and Len and the horses."

His eyes lit up, and he pulled the contraption onto his head. She knew how to manage him like no one else could, that was the thing. Mam and Tom could calm him down and cheer him along, but only his Maysie – her presence – made him feel completely safe. It had been so, Mam said, ever since his moon face had peered over the edge of the cradle and seen her newborn self, crinkled and kicking. Mostly, she liked it, the importance of it, but sometimes having him always with her was like someone was holding her ever so lightly by the throat so she couldn't quite swallow.

As Mrs. Walton led them out onto the stage, Davey let out a wail when he saw all the people looking up from the church hall chairs, but the clapping drowned it out. Although it was afternoon, the curtains were drawn in the hall, shutting out the sunshine, and the room smelled dusty like an attic or a hayloft. There were all the familiar faces – Dr. Yates, Mrs. Coulter, and Mrs. Miller and Mrs. Brown, who kept house together with Mrs. Miller's crippled daughter. At the front sitting next to the Vicar was Lady Sherwood, wearing a beautiful cream-coloured dress and a very large hat.

Mrs. Walton said some words to the audience, but May heard nothing because she was going to have to recite a poem, and no one had told her all the faces would be looking up like this in the dusky hall, row upon row of them. First, Mrs. Craddock, the Vicar's wife, played some chords on the piano, and all the children straggled into a song they'd practiced with Mrs. Walton giving them encouraging looks, and pulling funny faces as she mouthed the words, her hands beating time in the air. Then it was the turn of two blackface boys in pleated paper collars that made them scratch their necks. They shuffled their feet and began to sing in very quiet voices, "Swing low, sweet chariot coming for to carry me home," and May saw a beautiful white carriage with golden facings swayed gently on its axle as four white horses drew it down a road towards the setting sun. She was so completely captivated by the vision of the chariot that she didn't notice when the song was over, and the people were clapping, and suddenly there was Mrs. Walton beckoning her to step forward to the front of the stage.

May glanced down at the smiling faces of Mam and Mrs. Coulter, but wished she hadn't because she was going to let them down, let everybody down, because her mind was a blank. She couldn't remember one word of the poem, the words that she'd so carefully practiced and practiced till they unrolled one after the other like a long carpet, but not now. Her mind was a great white sheet in the humming silence of the big church hall where the upturned faces waited.

Then as her eyes found Mrs. Walton's face and saw her mouthing the opening words, May's mind caught hold and the lines began to come. She fixed her gaze on the small round window at the back of the hall so she wouldn't have to see the faces and told the poem to that high circle of light. After a verse or two, her body relaxed, and she was able to enjoy the sound of her voice, the only voice – hers – in a room full of people. Time was suspended as May hung there in her moment, but as she started the last stanza, she once again heard the rustling of the audience and the fidgets of the other children and saw Mrs. Walton's smile urging her on.

Britannia needs no bulwarks,
No towers along the steep,
Her march is o'er the mountain waves,
Her home is on the deep.
With thunders from her native oak,

May raised her voice in a crescendo for the climax and drew up at the end of the last line like a racehorse who'd given his all. Up went the hands of the spectators – her mother's laughing face, Dr. Yates calling "Hurrah," and Reverend Craddock inclining his head towards Lady Sherwood, who was smiling and patting her grey-gloved hands together.

The rest of the show tilted swiftly towards its climax, a tableau of Empire where they all waved Union Jacks as Ada walked across the stage in her glorious blue eiderdown and a slightly crooked paper crown. May set her face and refused to smile. The applause surged as Mrs. Walton came up on the stage and made a bow. Her hands went up to her cheeks with surprise as Reverend Craddock came forward with a bunch of irises tied with a gold ribbon. May remembered the exact same thing had happened at the Christmas pageant, but Mrs. Walton accepted the flowers as if they were the most splendid surprise in the world.

Then up stood Lady Sherwood, ushered by the Vicar up onto the stage, her skirts dusting the wooden steps. One by one Mrs. Walton called forward the children to collect their prizes. "For recitation and nature study, May Hallam" and May edged her way past her classmates and reached for the dictionary held out to her in a gloved hand, remembering at the last minute to crook her knee. She'd kept her eyes on the boards of the stage, but she was sorry when it was Ada's turn to get the needlework prize. Lady Sherwood bent towards her smiling and saying something that May couldn't hear, and Ada said something back, and May knew that could have been her if she'd had the courage to look up and look the great lady in the eye.

Back at the schoolhouse Mrs. Walton dismissed class for the summer and May gathered up her satchel, heavy with her prize book. She waited for Davey as the other children pushed past each other to get out of the door. As he slowly put his pencils into his satchel and fastened every buckle, May gazed around the room at the map of the Empire, the King's photograph, the globe, the ink jug, and the cane on Mrs. Walton's desk and wondered if they would look different once she'd been away.

Mrs. Walton followed May and Davey out of the schoolhouse, turning to lock the door. Calling "Good afternoon, children," she got on her bicycle and pedalled off down the lane. As May watched her narrow back and neat straw hat disappear down the lane, she remembered that there'd once been a time when she'd overheard talk about sending Davey away. For a week or two, she'd lain awake every night, her stomach in a terrible twist thinking of him going somewhere she wouldn't be able to protect him. In the end, he was allowed to stay because Mrs. Walton told the School Board she'd give him extra lessons. Despite the lessons, he still struggled, but at least he was learning.

They passed Ada in the lane, talking to some of the other girls who held their satchels against their chests like shields and laughed behind their hands at Davey. Ada didn't laugh, but when the girls turned and walked away, she walked with them.

May felt the sun on her lids when she closed her eyes and turned her face up to it. Davey tapped her arm. "Maysie, do you think they'll be there? Even today?"

"Probably. We could go around the long way, but then we won't have time to go up to Home Farm before tea. We don't have to go if you'd rather not."

Knowing she was going to have to leave him, May was ready to let Davey have his way in everything, even though her stomach bloated with anticipation.

Davey sighed. "But I want to see the horses."

"All right then."

She braced her shoulders to be ready for the gauntlet she knew she'd have to run.

As expected, when they reached the edge of the village, boys burst from the hedge, their faces shiny soup plates, their black mouths open, whooping and yodelling. Davey's hands flew to his ears, and he wailed. May pushed him behind her, keeping her eye on Reggie Arkwright, the ringleader, the biggest boy in the school. She knew they'd only shove and threaten, but, like always, it made the sick come up into her throat.

"Go away, you big bullies."

One boy tried to reach around May to grab Davey. She pushed him back, but then Reggie came at them, jostling May with his belly, pushing at her with his hips.

"What's the matter, mongol boy – hiding behind your little sister?"

She smelled his dank breath and felt a speck of his spit hit her face. Yanking the satchel off her shoulder, she swung it hard at Reggie's head, and he fell backwards, a trickle of blood sliding from his ear. He looked as astonished as May felt. The other boys stepped back, mouths open, and she grabbed Davey's arm and they ran.

By the time they reached the towpath, May knew the boys wouldn't follow. She'd come to know how far they'd go and how to wait them out, but she'd never fought back before. It was because of the poem, the hush that had fallen as she'd spoken those words – it had made her feel a power she hadn't known she had. She bent over gasping with laughter. The dictionary that came from the grey-gloved hands of Lady Sherwood had just knocked Reggie Arkwright for six.

"It's all right, Davey. They're gone."

He whimpered a few more times, but she pointed to a water rat plopping into the canal, and he forgot the boys in an instant. The towpath was lush with white stitchwort, oxeye daisies, and the spikes of foxgloves, and starry twigs of elderflower were bright all along the bank. Midges hovered over the lazy water, and gnats swarmed a fresh pile of droppings from a barge horse.

Above them, poplars pointed to the sky. Willows bent towards the water, trailing across the path. May held back their tendrils for Davey to step through, and he laughed as the softness brushed his face. She spotted a heron standing motionless on the opposite bank. Just as she reached to nudge Davey to show him, she heard the whistle of a train over the fields and remembered how bad Davey had been on the morning Lily left home. She'd got a job as a housemaid at a place called Warrington Grange a long way down south. Her trunk had gone ahead on the baker's cart, but Mam, May, and Davey walked with her to Mummersford Halt to help her with her case.

"You'll have enough to do carrying it on the journey." Mam said, her voice sounding like she had something in her throat.

At the station, Davey whooped and cowered when the train wheezed up to the platform, covering his ears with his hands and Lily kissed him wherever she could find a space. A quick hug for May, and then she was holding Mam tightly, and Davey, sensing a great gulf opening, had started to scream.

"Come on, let's cut across the ley field."

"No, Maysie! What about the cows?"

"They won't hurt you. Come on."

She climbed over a stile and waited for Davey to clamber over after her. They skirted the edge of the field, the cattle looking up lazily as they passed. The grass smelled of sap and wild onions. They bent to watch the bees clinging to a patch of white clover, their tiny wings a blur, Davey's face rapt and slack, thinking of nothing but the bees. Would he be so easy to distract when she was gone? Their family was a tight circle, she and her brothers and sisters around Mam, and then outside that circle was a wider loop of people they knew – Aunt Emma, the Coulters, the Vicar and his wife. And beyond that circle came a ring of people they'd never seen before and then another and another, the circles getting bigger and bigger until the whole field was a world filled with strangers.

"Maysie! You're not listening!"

"What did you say?"

He stopped walking and rubbed his head. "Can't remember."

At the far end of the field, they climbed another stile into the lane leading to Home Farm. The butcher's cart passed them, iron wheels rattling, and Mr. Bowen called hello. The dry stream bed was a mass of cow parsley, and a smell of wild thyme rose from somewhere. A heap of stones lay on the verge, ready for the road menders. At a turn in the lane, there was a thinning place in the hedge, and they bent down low to see the great house, a long expanse of stone the colour of milky custard, rising out of its parkland like something that had always been there. Thin lines of smoke rose from the chimneys.

"How many rooms do you think there are?" Davey always whispered when he talked of the big house or the family.

"A thousand. At least."

"But who lives in them all?" His mouth was wet and slurry next to her ear.

"Servants, mostly. And they have rooms for people who visit the family. See how the flag's flying? That's how we know the family's there."

"We already know! We saw her today."

At the end of the lane, they climbed the gate and jumped down into the farmyard, passing the midden with its buzzing cloud of flies and stopping to watch the swifts diving into their nests under the eaves, the neat, tightly packed ovals with the perfectly round hole for a door. The stable smelled of straw and horse piss, tickly to the nose. There was no one in sight, but they heard the clang of zinc buckets being filled with water, the hiss of grain poured into a trough, a burst of neighing and a hoarse wheezy bark.

"Someone's got croup," May said. "Maybe it's Birdie. Tom said she was off her feed."

No one was in the harness room. On the distempered walls, greening with damp, hung the massive harnesses for the ploughs and the hay waggons. And ranged along the splintering wooden shelves were large clear bottles of embrocation and stoppered red and green glass jars labelled "linseed," "vinegar," and "turpentine."

"It's feeding time – they're all in the stalls."

And as they turned, there was Len behind them, with looping tangles of reins, bridles, and tethers hanging from both upheld hands. "Eh up, you two. Up to no good?"

Len, with his fair silky hair always falling forward over his eyes, the shy one next to Tom's brazen charm. The gentle one, the one who spoke little but never shirked a task or spoke angrily. How could she live without Len for a month, so far away from his gentle comfortable presence? Again, the stab of anxiety in her gut and a momentary sense of falling.

Len stood Davey up on a chair and let him hang the bridles, patiently telling him which one went on which hook. May stood close to Len's side, breathing in his scent of hay, liniment, and leather. It kept their father with them, that smell on her brothers, like his pipe resting on the window ledge beside his chair, and his gaiters hanging on the back of the scullery door. How did Lily bear it down south, so far away from all the smells and sounds of home?

May turned away. "Where's Tom?"

"With Raven."

Walking down the row of stalls, she stopped to reach up to a giant Shire who bent to smell her head and nibble at her hair. "Are you hungry, Princess? Your dinner's coming." May felt the velvet moistness of the mare's nose against the side of her head and pulled away before her ear was gripped between those long hard teeth.

A stable boy came along the row, leaning sideways with the weight of the bucket he was carrying.

"Hello, Fred."

"Eh up, Missy. What you doing up here?"

"Last day of school."

"Course it is. That brother of yours with you?"

"With Len, putting tack away."

"Regular apprentices you and him be. We'll have you working here as soon as you turn fourteen."

It was a joke of course. They all thought the horses were too powerful for a girl. Tom had laughed so loud and hard when she'd said she wanted to be a waggoner that she'd hated him for days afterwards.

About to lift the latch on Raven's stall door, she saw his shiny black hindquarters lift up, and he let loose a stream of steaming-hot piss that bubbled on the straw. Tom laughed as she slid into the stall. "Just missed a spring shower, Maybelle."

"Very funny."

She slid her hand along Raven's warm flank so he'd know she was there. "Was that Birdie coughing?"

"Aye. It's not croup yet, but Stan's putting a linseed poultice on her chest just in case."

"Poor Birdie." She stood up on tiptoe to stroke Raven's muscular neck and gather a handful of his rough mane.

"She'll be all right."

There was a hardness to Tom that always surprised May. Once when she was quite small, she and Davey had come upon him crying because Mam had shown him how to wring a chicken's neck, but he hadn't done it well and the hen had suffered. But those were the last tears she'd ever seen him shed. He'd taught her a lot about horses – how to clean a wound with warm salt water and put turpentine on a sore that wouldn't heal. How to make a poultice of sugar water and aloe to wrap over a horse's scrape or blister.

"May, hold his halter for a jif. He fidgets something awful when I do his hooves."

Tom bent over and hauled up each shaggy black hoof at a time to chip out the hardened mud. Slivers of dirt peppered May's legs as she held onto the halter and rubbed Raven's nose.

"Mam says I'm to visit Lily at her place."

"Is that right?"

"Davey's not to know yet. He'll not be happy."

"Don't fret about him, Maysie. He needs to learn to do without you for a bit."

"Ada won't take care of him – she never does."

"Don't be so hard on her. You and Davey are like twins – she's got no one. Anyway, I'll keep an eye out for him. We'll play horse-shoes and go hunting for mushrooms."

"He'll like that. I hope he'll be all right."

"He'll manage. And you'll have lots to tell him when you get home. Maybe I'll teach Davey to ride Mam's bicycle – his legs are long enough now. Not like you, short-arse."

She wanted to say, "Do I have to go?" but she knew what the answer was. Appealing to Tom would get her nowhere. He and she both knew that Mam made the decisions, and her mind was made up.

She left Tom grooming Raven's coat and went back along the row of stalls to the feed room. Davey was helping Len to mix the horses' mash, holding the long paddle and stirring. He looked at May, his bright, unknowing face turned to her like she was the sun, and she had to step out into the yard and slap her hands against the rough stone wall to stop herself from crying.

CHAPTER 13

July 1914

The train galloped like a racehorse, the trees, cows, farms going by too fast for May to see them properly. She kept turning to look back at things and missing what came next. And Mrs. Craddock called this one "the slow train."

Now she thought of it, her legs were no longer shaking. She felt a shudder of sorrow about what she'd left behind, but there was too much to look at and everything that was happening required her full attention.

The parting had been terrible. Davey had started to get upset the night before when he saw Mam packing the carpet bag, but until he saw May put on her hat, he hadn't known she was the one who was leaving. Mrs. Coulter had to hustle her out of the house, but May could still hear his screams as they walked past the pond. She hoped Mrs. Coulter wouldn't say anything kind or she'd cry. Or run back home and face the wrath of Mam.

There was nothing for it. She'd had to go on. By the time they reached the Vicarage where Reverend Craddock had the gig waiting to drive his wife and May to the railway station, she had herself mostly under control.

The train ran alongside the river, which lazed in the half-light of the cloudy day. May saw a doe bend its head to drink, and Mrs.

Craddock tapped her arm to point out a gig and pair waiting by the railway gates for the train to pass, the horses jibbing at the noise and steam.

Then there were houses, first a few and then many close together and then a sudden blackness fell outside the window and May gasped till Mrs. Craddock explained they were in a tunnel under the streets of Nottingham. And then with great screeching of brakes, the train slowed and came to rest under a huge glass roof so dirty it shut out the sky.

A porter opened the door of their compartment and touched his cap brim.

"Where to, Ma'am?"

"The London train. Bags are in the guards' van – name of Craddock."

"Very good, Ma'am. Back in a jiffy."

May walked beside Mrs. Craddock down a long grey platform behind a porter pushing a trolley bearing Mrs. Craddock's cases with May's shabby carpet bag perched on top. The din was louder than anything she'd ever heard before, clanging, roaring engines, piercing whistles, the whoosh of escaping steam under the vast roof. People's lips were moving, but May couldn't hear what they said. Men and women pushed past each other, some running, and porters narrowly missed crashing into each other with their piled-up barrows. How could anyone not get lost in such a crush? May stayed as close to Mrs. Craddock's side as she dared without being too familiar. Mam had told her several times what an honour it was to be travelling with the Vicar's wife and how she must try to do everything to please her.

The porter came to a stop beside a train carriage that had a large number 1 on the shiny door. He held it open and handed them in. This carriage was plusher than the previous one. The seats felt like velvet and the woodwork shone. The porter lifted Mrs. Craddock's hat box and umbrella up onto the rack and wedged a large hamper underneath the seat. After he left the carriage, May leaned forward to watch him weave his trolley like a dancer through the crowd. Mrs. Craddock sank down on the seat opposite and exhaled a puff of air that was half a sigh and half a gasp, "There now, we're settled." And suddenly May realised that even the Vicar's wife was daunted by the journey.

There was a shrill whistle from somewhere and then a jolt, and the platform began to slide backwards away from the train. May almost cried out until she realised the train was moving, not the station. She felt silly and glanced over at Mrs. Craddock in case she'd noticed, but she was busy tugging her gloves off, finger by finger.

Back they plunged into a tunnel, and a sudden smell of soot oozed through the cracks around the window. When brightness returned, they were moving slowly between high banks of over-grown weeds and brambles and great bushes of Queen Anne's lace. Then a gasworks and a large lake with a man rowing a boat with a brown dog standing in the prow, its nose into the wind. Then the train picked up speed, and the world became a speeding blur once again.

They ate delicious cold chicken legs and ham sandwiches from the hamper. May felt obliged to refuse second helpings because Mam wouldn't want her to seem greedy. After the hamper had been packed away, Mrs. Craddock went very quiet and soon a gentle purring signalled she was asleep. May wanted to keep looking at the new and strange country beyond the window, but the rocking of the train made her eyes close of their own accord. She woke with a start from a dream of Davey when a guard tapped on the glass of the partition and asked Mrs. Craddock for their tickets. Confused not to wake up in her own bed, May was suddenly swept with panic. So many hours had passed since she'd left home and so many miles. How could she ever find her way home from here?

There had never been a time in her life when Davey hadn't been there. She thought she could remember the full moon of his face peering over the edge of her baby basket, and his hand reaching for hers across Mam's lap as each straddled a knee. He was her other half, her older twin. As long as the sun was up, they were together, and after dark they were parted only by the thin wall between the girls' room and the room where Davey slept with Tom and Len.

The astonishment of London distracted her from brooding. At first there was just the station, but then Mrs. Craddock waved away the motor taxis and hailed a hansom. May was thrilled by the little wooden apron that folded over their laps and the familiar smell of horse sweat and leather. They trotted out into the astonishment of the Euston Road. The tall buildings, so many people and drays and carts and motor cars and omnibuses and always a sourness at the back of her throat that Mrs. Craddock said was petroleum. And everywhere people jostled in the streets, all too close together, and the buildings close together too, looming over the streets. How could they find enough air to breathe? Yet people seemed to like it. She saw a cluster of women in boyish caps standing at a bus stop laughing so loud she could see into their open mouths.

Then once again they were in a railway carriage, this time on the Eastbourne train, shared with a lady in a large hat, a young man whose dark eyes kept darting towards the lady, and a man in a white collar like the Vicar's, who soon began an animated conversation with Mrs. Craddock when he learned her husband held the Mummersford living. He'd kindly given up his seat by the window to May so she kept her face turned to the passing fields. She saw a carthorse pulling a waggon down a long yellow field, a man holding the reins loosely, and for a second May missed her father so much she could barely breathe. The sky south of London was a cool blue with great heaps of white cloud, but she could see the shadows of the copses growing longer. It felt like they'd been travelling for days.

She almost cried with relief when the train pulled up at Ring-hampton station – with a clock made of flowers on the embank-ment – and saw Lily in her familiar old hat waiting by the ticket office. The clerical man helped May to jump down from the high

step and called a porter to collect her carpet bag from the guards'
van. Lily came towards her, relief and delight on her face, and
May ran to her. Lily turned her around quickly before she could
forget her manners, and together they called out their thanks to
Mrs. Craddock who smiled and waved a gloved hand from the
window.

And then she was walking down a cool lane overhung with
trees, hand in hand with her sister and, though she was still a long
way from home, a bit of her home was here, and it wasn't so
strange anymore.

Warrington Grange wasn't fancy. Nothing like Mummersford
Hall, more like a grander version of the Vicarage. Its brick walls
were furred with ivy, and the slate roof was the mossy grey of a
dove's wing. The best part was the long lawn that led down to the
head of a valley at the end of which lay a hazy blue line.

"Is that the sea I can smell?" she asked Lily.

"Isn't it the grandest thing?"

May nodded, though from that distance it didn't look much
bigger than the Trent.

They went in through the back door, which opened straight
into the kitchen. The room was full of juicy baking smells that
made the saliva rise in May's mouth.

"So this is the wee parcel you've been to fetch." A tall woman
with strong arms was stirring something in a pan on the range,
and as she turned to smile, May saw that she was missing one
front tooth.

"This is Mrs. Goodwin, May. She rules us all."

The woman made her shoulders go up and down as if she
were laughing. "Come and sit down and have a rock cake.
Connie's just this minute put them to cool. You too, Lil. You'll not
be needed upstairs for another half an hour."

A girl not much older than May came from the scullery, her

hands dripping. She had red hair and a wide nose. "Hello there. Lil, can you pour the tea? It's been mashing for you. I'm washing the lunch pots or I'd do it."

May couldn't stop staring at Connie's lashless eyes and freckles. Lily brought tea and a plate of the still-warm rock cakes. May was very hungry and eating gave her something to do that didn't require her to talk to these new people. As she was picking the raisins out of her second rock cake, a stout man dressed in striped trousers and a black cut-away jacket came through a swinging door.

"Miss Hallam, I presume?" he asked in a strong but melodic Scottish accent, bowing a little stiffly from the waist. "You're very welcome, but I trust you'll not get underfoot in the coming days. There's plenty wanting doing. Lily will show you the way."

And he picked up a tray of glasses and carried them away.

"Was that Mr. Birmingham?" she asked, and Lily and Connie burst out laughing.

Mrs. Goodwin said, "She's a green one."

Lily squeezed May's elbow. "Maysie, that was Mr. Moncrieff. He's the butler. He seems strict, but he's all right."

May asked Lily in a low voice, hoping not to be made fun of again. "How many other people are there?"

Lily had just taken a bite of rock bun so Mrs. Goodwin answered for her as she reached around them for a measuring spoon. "There's Tessa. She's a housemaid like your sister – she's on her day off just at the moment. And there's young Mr. Avery who's the master's valet as well as his chauffeur. And Mr. Noakes out in the garden."

May counted in her head. "Seven people to take care of one man. When you were with the Vicar and Mrs. Craddock, there was only you, a cook, and a groom."

Lily raised an eyebrow. "Wait till he has a house party. Then you'll see."

～

Mrs. Craddock had promised to send Mam a telegram from Brighton to let her know of May's safe arrival, but May couldn't wait to write Davey a long letter to tell him all about the trains and about the house and the interesting garden she could see from the window of Lily's attic bedroom. As Lily was putting May's things away in the press, Tessa came in, hat on the back of her head, hair coming loose.

"So, this your sister, Lil? How d'you do, miss?"

"Hello." May held out her hand to be shaken, but Tessa didn't seem to notice.

Bending to put May's spare pinafore in a drawer, Lily asked, "Where'd you go, then? Was he there?"

Tessa struck a pose, one hand on her waist, the other behind her head. "I should say so. Took me for a slap-up meal, full roast beef and Yorkshire, I'll have you know. Showed him my appreciation down below the sea front. Twice actually."

Lily shook her head and glanced towards May.

"Oops, pardon my loose tongue." Tessa threw off her hat and fell backwards on her bed. "My feet – oof. So, Miss May, how old are you?"

May paused in handing her folded underthings to Lily. "I'm eight."

"Ugh, they start them young in service in your family."

May looked from Tessa to Lily and back again and saw from Lily's expression that this girl was not her sister's friend.

May was to sleep on a mattress on the floor between Lily and Tessa's beds. The thought of mice running across the floor made her uneasy, but Tessa laughed and said the house was full of traps, and the rat catcher came once a week to empty and reset them.

"They never get as far as up here."

Even so, when she lay down and Lily turned off the electric light, May couldn't help listening for scratching, but all she heard was the squeak of a bicycle on the road beyond the gate and a soft far-off shushing that she thought might be the sea. They were not the noises of home. What if Davey woke in the night and came to find her, but there was just old Ada in that big bed, sleeping like a rock.

Her heart beat hard against the mattress so she turned on her back, looking up at the unfamiliar shadows, and felt the movement of the train underneath her, the sleepy feeling of the rhythm, the warmth through the window, Mrs. Craddock's purring snores, and then suddenly there was loud birdsong outside the window and Tessa's bare feet landed on her legs.

"Get up, lazybones."

As May struggled up from the floor, Lily emptied their chamber pots into a slop bucket and gestured to May to splash her face in the washbasin. Tessa was pulling on stockings that had holes in the toes. May thought she was dressing quickly, but both girls were ready before her and she had to rush to follow them. As they went in single file down the back stairs, she thought of what Mam had told her. "This is not a holiday. You're to learn everything you can about service for when your turn comes."

In the kitchen, Connie was stoking the range, her eyebrows dark with coal dust, and Mrs. Goodwin was kneading the dough for the day's bread. Lily and Tessa put on heavy cotton aprons, and Lily found an extra one for May.

"I'll do the library. You can have the drawing room and dining room," Tessa said.

It didn't seem fair to May that Lily had two rooms to Tessa's one, but Lily didn't argue. She picked up a basket full of tins, rags, and dusters, and May followed her along the dark corridor to the swing door, noticing the mouse traps along the wainscoting.

In the wide cheerful drawing room, Lily pulled back the curtains and tied them in place, pinching the fabric so that it fell just right. The rising sun slid in the room and lay across the carpet that swirled with blues, golds, and creams. May wasn't sure what needed to be cleaned because everything looked so crisp and shiny. She thought of home, the stains and scratches of everything, the dinge and fade of the walls, and wanted to be there so badly it was hard to take a breath.

"The first thing to do is check the wood basket is well stocked," Lily said. "You're lucky you're here in the summer. The master only has a fire in the drawing room if it's a chilly evening or he has company."

The sticks lay crossed and tidy in the hearth, the logs stacked neatly underneath.

"But we still have to polish the fender." Lily laid a cloth on the hearth and showed May how to tip the Reckitt's Brasso onto a rag and rub it into the brass. It was satisfying for a while, but then May's knees hurt, and she sat back and watched Lily push and pull a long-handled brush across the wooden floorboards. "What's that thing?"

"It's a donkey. It's got beeswax on it."

"Can I have a go?"

Lily held out the handle to her. "Be careful not to get any on the edge of the carpet."

The air felt as solid as the furniture in the room, and May longed for a window to be opened, but she could tell that wouldn't happen from Lily's determined posture as she dusted the side tables, the delicate ornaments, the thick piles of magazines.

"Hurry with that donkey. I've the dining room to do next. Can you dust the banisters? From the top down, and if you hear the master stirring, get out of sight."

As the clock in the hallway struck eight, they were back in the kitchen, where Mrs. Goodwin had the master's breakfast tray ready to take up. "Sit down, girls. Connie's bringing the porridge."

It was creamier than the kind Mam made, and May was comforted by its warmth.

When the dandyish valet, Mr. Avery, came to report that Mr. Birmingham had come downstairs, Lily and May carried the cleaning things up the back stairs to the bedrooms. Tessa said she'd be right with them after she'd helped Connie with the slops, and May saw Lily roll her eyes. "Have a cigarette more like."

The master's bedroom was large, with long sash windows looking down the valley towards the sea. It had a different smell from the rest of the house, not unpleasant, a musky, smoky essence that rose from the unmade bed.

"Stop gawking. We haven't got long to get this done – he could come up at any minute." Lily knelt down to empty the ashes from the grate into a bucket, and, as she began to lay a new fire, May said, "Let me do that. I'm the best fire maker in the family, have you forgotten?"

Lily laughed. "Hurry up then," she said, running a duster over the twisted mahogany of the bed posts. After washing their hands in the master's echoey bathroom, which was tiled all the way up to the ceiling and had a real toilet with a chain to pull, they stripped the sheets off his bed, tumbling them into a heap on the floor, and stretched a fresh one across the mattress. Lily showed May how to do hospital corners, tucking them under like the folds of a brown paper parcel, and then came the top sheet and the blankets, perfectly even on all sides, followed by the soft eiderdown and the plumped-up pillows in fresh new pillowcases. May stood back to admire the made-up bed and longed to fall face first into its crisp softness.

On the landing, Lily strained to listen for noises from downstairs and hearing nothing, beckoned May to follow her into a room at the front of the house. "We'll just take a peek."

It was a sweet little sitting room, with chintz chairs in a summery print and a red velvet chaise beside the wide bow window.

"Oh, how lovely," May said, gazing at the shepherdess figurines and flower vases and the view of green fields in the valley where she longed to run.

"This room's for his wife, once he has one," Lily said, checking an ornament for dust.

"Why doesn't he have one now?"

"Mr. Avery says the master's happy as he is. And it's just as well for us. We have it easy here, you know. If there was a mistress, some people would have to change their ways."

"You mean Tessa?"

Lily glanced towards the door. "She gets away with murder. Even Mr. Moncrieff's a bit afraid of her. Once she told him he was a dried-up old haggis, and all he did was go bright red and walk away."

The midday dinner was a good surprise – a joint of lamb, crunchy roast potatoes, and sweet peas with lashings of rich gravy. Lily warned May not to linger because as soon as Mr. Moncrieff put his knife and fork together, the rest of them had to finish as well. May didn't need telling twice.

She barely had a chance to digest the roly-poly and custard when they were off again, taking advantage of the master's absence in Brighton to lift up the carpets from the entrance hall. While Lily scrubbed the exposed tiles on her hands and knees, Tessa and May carried the carpets outside and hung them over the washing line. This was something May knew how to do, hitting the carpets with the beater and watching the dust rise in clouds from the warp and weft till her armpits grew damp. Tessa leaned against the doorframe and watched her, a cigarette between her fingers, her hair rising out of its pins.

May was glad to be outside, even with the carpet dust. Back indoors, when Lily set her to rubbing away tiny corners of tarnish in a fancy silver teapot, her spirits fell. She wished she was hunting mushrooms in Mummersford Wood with Davey or riding high on Raven's back as Tom led him out from between the shafts, the harness warm and leathery under her hands.

There was a lull when tea was brewed and they all sat around the big kitchen table eating seed cake with gooseberry jam, except for Mr. Moncrieff who was said to be decanting the wine in the butler's pantry. "But he's probably having a snooze," Tessa said, laughing behind her hand.

Mr. Avery had bought a newspaper when he took the master

to Brighton and was reading out loud about an air race between London and Paris. "The American Walter Brock won in a time of just over seven hours for the return trip, beating French aviator Roland Garros, whilst the Irish Peer Lord Carbery ditched in the English Channel and was rescued."

"Beaten by a Yankee and a Froggie? Shame on him!" Tessa said, her mouth full of cake, her hair standing out on either side of her cap.

Mrs. Goodwin poured herself another cup from the large brown teapot. "They're mad. Imagine being up that high! It's not natural."

Connie shuddered, her chin on her freckled fist. "You'd never get me up there."

With a rustle, Mr. Avery turned to another page. "It's the coming thing though. It says here there's been a new record set – the first continuous flight of over 24 hours."

Under cover of the general conversation, May whispered to Lily, "When do we get to be outside?"

Lily whispered back, "Not till our afternoon off."

"That's all?"

This was awful news. Not to be outside at the height of summer. To wade through long grass, lie under trees and watch the branches heave and toss. The air in the kitchen felt too dense to breathe even with the back door open.

Soon there was the bustle before dinner, the need to light the fires in the library and the dining room and to slot new candles in the silver candlesticks as Mr. Moncrieff carefully laid one place at the table, the trio of wine glasses catching the evening light. And helping out in the kitchen, putting out the cutlery for the servants' evening meal, cold chicken and bread and butter, she and Lily going to and fro while Tessa sat at the end of the kitchen table taking her time, peeling an apple into one long twisting skin. After helping Connie by drying the pots and dishes, Lily and Tessa sat down with the mending basket. May was tired, but she drew up a chair next to them and slotted a thimble on her middle finger. Lily looked at her over the sock she was darning. "You've never been any good at needlework. Why don't you go up to bed?"

May couldn't stop herself from yawning. "Would it be all right if I stepped out into the garden for a minute?"

Lily glanced at Mrs. Goodwin, who looked up from writing in the margin of her fat recipe book with a gap-toothed smile. "Oh, let the child go out. Just stay away from the library windows, May. Do you know where those are?"

May nodded and slipped off the chair and out of the back door. She leaned back against the wall in the cool air, looking up at the fading sky above the dark green trees, an ache in her stomach. There'd been no time to write Davey a letter, and it seemed there wouldn't be for days. A dull ache of worry for him bloomed like a cloud of evening stock and jasmine and trailed its scent across the gravel.

Mrs. Goodwin never missed a chance to choose May to run down the drive to meet the butcher's boy or cut long-stemmed flowers for the drawing room vases, and May understood she meant to be kind, but sometimes it made it worse to have only those few minutes in the open air. One morning Mrs. Goodwin sent her out to pick peas in the kitchen garden, and as she went down the rows snapping off the pods, May heard the hard sound of metal striking wood. She peered over the low hedge and saw Mr. Noakes, the gardener, looking into the shed where the lawn pony was kept.

Another clang. She made her way round the hedge and, looking through the half-door of the stable, saw Mr. Noakes edging round the inside of the loose box with the harness as the pony threw his head up, ears back. Whenever the gardener got too close, the animal gave the stall another kick. May could see the splintered wood where the hoof had struck.

"What's the matter with him, Mr. Noakes?"

"Damned if I know. He was a-okay yesterday, but he seems to have got the jitters today. Just when the lawn wants cutting."

"Something's got him riled."

"You think so?"

She could hear the sarcasm in the elderly man's voice but also the weariness. "Doesn't matter what it is, he needs fixing."

"What nonsense are you talking, girl? He just needs a good clout."

The pony gave the wall another mighty whack, and Mr. Noakes fled from the stall, bolting the half-door behind him.

"Has he got any sores or scrapes?" she asked him.

"Not that I've seen."

"Has he ever been this way before?"

"Not a once." Mr. Noakes looked down at May. "What do you know about horses anyway?"

"My brothers are waggoners, and my father was a waggoner too."

"Is that right?" Noakes scratched the tuft of hair that seeped from under his cap. "Well, what do you advise, missy? I'm stumped. Plants I know about, but horses are a mystery."

"I reckon it's his mouth. He seems afraid of the bit."

Mr. Noakes looked at the pony, who was eyeing them over his shoulder. "Hm, you might be onto something there. He hasn't eaten any hay, and that's not like the little bugger. Look at the belly on him – he likes his feed."

"What's his name?"

"Benjy."

May rested her chin on the rough top of the stable half-door and crooned to the pony, "There's my little man, my good boy, Benjy."

A string of saliva dropped from the pony's mouth to the straw. She turned to Noakes. "It's definitely his mouth."

She handed the bowl of peas to Noakes and slid back the bolt on the half-door.

"Be careful, missy." Though he sounded anxious, he didn't try to stop her from going in.

"Who's my good boy, my good little man, there's a good boy." She edged her way round to his head, the pony watching her, his ears flicking. "There, there, good boy. No one's going to hurt you, nooo."

The pony looked at her out of the corner of his eye, then swung his head around to sniff her. He was a Welsh cob, small enough for May to see over his back. She stood stock-still and let his rubbery lips, slick with drool, nibble at the edge of her pinafore. She raised her hand slowly, palm out, and he let her stroke the white stripe on his nose. His ears rolled forward. She rubbed the soft space between his nostrils, and he snuffled, his eyes half closing. May let him enjoy the rubbing for a moment and then, cupping his chin in her hand, gently pulled down his lower lip in her thumb and finger. Before he yanked his head back, she'd seen an oozing sore on the mottled shellfish pink of his gum.

She began crooning again, and the pony lowered his head and let her go back to stroking his nose. In the same sing-song voice, she spoke to Mr. Noakes, "Poor Benjy's got a mouth ulcer. On his gum. Has he eaten any buttercups?"

"Buttercups? I don't know. I suppose he might have nibbled one or two in the paddock. What should I do, miss?"

She saw that Noakes was more than ready to listen to her advice. He'd even taken off his cap. "It needs to be bathed in salted water and then a comfrey poultice. And he'd better not have a bit till it heals."

Mr. Noakes snorted. "Who's going to pull the mower? The master won't like it if the grass gets long."

May looked at him across the pony's flank. She had no answer. All she knew about was horses. "Do you want me to get the salted water, Mr. Noakes?"

"No, no, you stay with the animal. I'll fetch it."

"Would you give the peas to Mrs. Goodwin as you go?"

"Yes'm, I will."

From the warm hay-smelling gloom of the stall, May heard his boots clomp away towards the house. The pony nudged her in the chest, and she moved around to lay her face against his neck, breathing in his sweat and leather smell. As he turned his head and tried to put his nose in her pocket, she was dizzy with longing for home.

❧

As Lily and May came indoors from the ash pit, Mrs. Goodwin said, "Lil, the master wants to see you – and her," pointing to May with a flour-covered finger.

Lily turned to May, her face drained of colour. "What have you done?"

The adults' faces were grim, and May felt a cold shiver between her shoulders. "I don't know!"

Tessa was smoking a cigarette just outside the open back door. "I told you it was a bad idea to have her here with you. You can't keep an eye on her every minute."

"Better hurry." Mrs. Goodwin nodded her head towards the door. "Mr. Moncrieff's waiting to take you in."

Lily untied May's apron and straightened her pinafore, then did the same to herself. Mr. Moncrieff put his head round the door from the butler's pantry. "There you are. Hurry up, we mustn't keep him waiting."

As they followed the butler through the house, May saw how Lily's red-knuckled hands shook and her face looked tight and scared, and May burped up some bile in her mouth and swallowed it down.

Mr. Walter Birmingham, a thin man with receding yellow hair and pale blue eyes, was standing at the mantelpiece in the library, smoking a cigarette. Two long sleek dogs lay on the hearth rug at his feet, one a tan colour with a white stripe down its breastbone and the other a brindled grey. Seeing Lily bob a curtsey, May did the same.

"So this is the famous young lady who fixed my lawn pony."

May glanced up at Lily who gripped her hands into fists and spoke. "Sir, I'm so very sorry if she's been a bother and been where she shouldn't when you've been so kind as to let her stay here. I'll make sure it never happens again, I promise on my honour, sir."

Lily's voice was shaking, but May found she'd stopped feeling afraid as soon as she'd seen the man, the smart cut of his clothes, the rich smell of his tobacco. There was something about him that felt comfortable and familiar, though she couldn't think why. He leaned on the mantelpiece and looked them up and down, first May, then Lily, and May looked right back, taking in his long white fingers, the tiny shaving cut on his chin. A trapped bluebottle rattled and buzzed between the panes of the upper and lower sash windows and, whenever it paused, the soft sounds of the dogs panting and Lily's heel fidgeting on the carpet.

Mr. Birmingham smiled. "Not at all. In fact, I'm thinking of taking her on as my new stable man. Not that one Welsh cob counts as a stable. Now I have the car, there's no need. More's the pity. You can't drive, can you?" he asked, looking at May.

She laughed. It seemed called for, though Lily nudged her with a sharp elbow. The grey dog got up and walked over on spindly legs to sniff May's pinafore. His ribs rose through his sleek fur, and his belly curved up to almost nothing between his back legs.

"Is he hungry, sir?"

Mr. Birmingham flicked his cigarette into the unlit fireplace. "I see your encyclopaedic knowledge of horses doesn't extend to dogs. They're meant to be that thin. See how shiny his coat is? That shows he's very healthy." The other dog ambled over and looked up at May with liquid oval eyes. "This one's Match and the other's Dash. They eat plenty of food, I assure you. Mr. Moncrieff prepares it with his own hands – kidneys, liver, hearts. It's all right – you can touch them if you like."

She'd hesitated, used only to the farm dogs with their fanged white teeth and matted coats, but as they pressed their noses into her hands, she bent to stroke their narrow heads and bony backs. Their fur was smooth, and she rubbed them behind their ears and on their haunches, making their back legs twitch and scratch in the air. She laughed and looked up at Lily, who was still standing, tensed and wary, and wouldn't meet her eyes.

Mr. Birmingham lit another cigarette. The bluebottle, having been silent for a while, began its frantic buzzing again. "So young May Hallam, are they making you work around the house? Turning you into a little skivvy, are they? A girl with talents like yours should make something of herself."

"I want to be a waggoner, sir. That's what I'd like best."

She saw Lily look towards the bluebottle, watching it bang against the glass.

"Why farm work? Why not study to become a veterinary doctor? You obviously have a knack for taking care of animals."

May didn't know what to say to that. The bluebottle buzzed and buzzed, and May itched to throw up the sash to let it fly out. Mr. Birmingham turned to his bookshelves and scanned the spines with one long finger. "Ah!" He drew out a blue volume with delicate gold edging. "Here's a book for a horse lover."

He held it out. May hesitated, glancing up at Lily.

"Come on then. I don't bite."

She stepped cautiously towards him and took the book. The title, *Black Beauty*, was written in gold curly letters.

"Do you have a strong stomach, Miss May Hallam?"

The question confused her. How could he know about the ball of air that inflated her belly whenever she was worried or upset? "I'm not sure, sir."

"Well, you'll need it. This is no fairy story. I want you to read it and tell me what you think of it. I don't want to hear of you doing any more skivvying. Don't you agree, Miss Lily?"

May saw Lily's face turn letterbox red.

"Whatever you think is right, sir," she said.

"I sense a reservation. Come on now, speak up."

Lily looked down at her shoes. "Our mam won't like it, sir. She wants our May to learn how to be in service."

"I see. All right then, how about she skivvies in the mornings but has the afternoons off? Would that satisfy your 'mam'?"

"Yes sir. Thank you, sir," Lily replied, eyes still down.

"All right then. And Miss May, I'd be much obliged if you'd keep an eye on that lawn pony of mine as well once in a while."

"Yes sir. Thank you, sir."

May curtsied, holding the large slippery book to her chest, and as she followed Lily to the door, she glanced back at Mr. Birmingham, but he had already turned away and was picking up the newspaper. In the corridor beyond the closed door, May stopped short. "That's who it is! He's like Dada."

Lily frowned, her face still a deep rich red. "What? There's nothing about him like Dada. Don't talk daft."

The next morning May threw herself into the cleaning, scrubbing the tiled floor of the Master's bathroom and scouring the bathtub with its funny lion feet, a job she knew Lily hated. After midday dinner, she stood around awkwardly, not knowing what to do, till Mr. Moncrieff looked at her over his glasses. "Well, off you go and enjoy yourself. Master's orders." She followed Lily into the scullery and watched her fill a sudsy bucket to go and scrub the boot room. "I'm sorry, Lil. I didn't know he'd say it."

Lily heaved the bucket out of the sink. "I don't care. It's what Mam'll think."

"But I'm learning about service every day – I am. She can't think I'm not."

Wiping her hands on her apron, Lily nodded her head towards the door. "Go on then. It'll be all right."

Somehow, this man with his funny teasing manner and his thin, beautiful dogs had known she couldn't be indoors hour after hour. She remembered the book he'd lent her and fetched it from the shelf next to the cookbooks.

"You take care of that, May." Mrs. Goodwin said. "It looks expensive. Don't you go getting it dirty."

"I won't."

With a skidding sound, the postman's bicycle pulled up outside the door, and he leaned in holding out a pile of letters.

"Can you get those for me, pet?" Mrs. Goodwin asked May. "My hands are all over lard."

Right on top of the bundle there was a letter addressed to herself in Mam's curly handwriting. Her heart beating fast, she slid it off the pile and ran out into the kitchen garden to read it. Her hands shook as she broke the seal. What if there was bad news? What if Davey was ill with missing her? She saw him white-faced and blue around the eyes as he'd looked one time when he fell down the bank from Granny Maitland's garden.

Dear Maysie,

Lily's written to say you're fitting in well at Warrington Grange and working hard.

When had Lily found the time to write to Mam?

Len has a little cold but otherwise we are all well at home. Davey misses you, but he and Ada have been busy whitewashing the scullery. He gets more on himself than on the walls, but it keeps him out of trouble. And he and Ada go up to the stables each evening to walk home with the boys so you needn't worry yourself about him. Just be a good girl, and it'll not be long before you and Lily are back among us. Affectionately, Mam.

PS Give our Lil a kiss from me.

Ada. He was going to the stables with Ada and painting walls and not missing May at all.

Her stomach felt gassy and looking around to make sure no one heard, she let loose a fart to relieve the pressure. She folded up the letter and put it inside the book. The sun blazed off the greenhouse, and she felt its warmth coat her shoulders.

That afternoon she explored every field, every path, every hollow surrounding the Grange. She found abandoned birds' nests, windfall apples, and, near a high privet hedge, a drift and flutter of Red Admirals that brushed against her hair. And best of all, right in the middle of a fallow field behind the Grange, there was an oak tree, with gnarls and boles that made it easy to climb and a niche between two wide branches that was the perfect place to hide and hold the large blue book on her lap.

"The first place that I can well remember was a large, pleasant meadow with a pond of clear water in it." At first, she was confused about why the person speaking lived in a meadow, but when she understood that Black Beauty was a young colt telling his story, she gave her whole attention to the story.

She read about his first years and kind treatment by Squire Gordon, but then came Ginger and the check rein, her mouth frothing with blood, and Sir Oliver and his docked tail, cut through the flesh and bone, and May understood what the master had meant when he'd asked if she had a strong stomach. She closed the book, using Mam's letter to mark her place, and slid down the trunk to the ground. Through the patchy hedge that marked the Grange's garden, she saw Benjy plodding across the lawn in his rubber shoes with Mr. Noakes guiding the roller and was thankful his mouth had healed.

The next afternoon May walked down into the valley towards Ringhampton, but the roads were paved and hot beneath her boots and the fields were full of growing crops with no room to run across. Turning back, she stopped by the entrance gate to the Grange and counted its windows – twelve of them, and that was just at the front. Circling round the house, she made again for her special tree. The air was hot and full of insects and birdsong and, underneath, the growl of a distant motor car, and as she sat still and listened, May had the inside-out feeling of being completely alone with no Davey at her shoulder like a shadow. Davey, who loved Ada now like he used to love May.

She wondered what it would be like if there was another girl her age, a friend, in the tree with her, perhaps even the Master's daughter, which was nonsense because he had no daughter, but the more she thought about this girl, the more she felt her presence whoever she was, straddling a branch just the other side of the trunk.

"Hello?" she said, expecting no answer but at that instant she knew the girl's name was Tabbie and that was it. In her head, she talked to Tabbie about Mr. Birmingham and Tessa's jokes that only Tessa found funny and about Davey and how she worried about him but now wasn't sure she should. When she heard herself start to talk out loud, she felt foolish and went back to reading her book.

Black Beauty had been sold to a livery stable and May was anxious to know if he'd be treated well. She read on, turning the pages quickly, till something, a shift in the light, made her look up. The air was close, and as she peered out between the leaves, she saw the sky had turned a bruised lilac. Rain was coming, and May knew she had to get back to the house to stop the book from getting wet.

As she started to clamber down, the book clenched under one arm, she heard a strange noise from the far end of the field, and as she paused to listen, a baying mass of hounds crashed through a gap in the hedge and rushed across the field. The tree quivered under May's hands like the ground was shaking, and she saw a dozen horses and riders galloping straight towards her. As she clutched the trunk with both hands, terrified of falling, the book slipped loose, landed face down and was trampled by the wild blur of red, black, and brown.

In the sudden stillness, May clung to the tree, arms and legs shaking. She didn't dare look down. In the distance, she heard a horn blowing and the hounds barking. Slowly she climbed lower, looking carefully for any stragglers, but there seemed to be none.

As the rain began, she squatted and lifted up the muddy, broken book, its cover branded with a horseshoe, and the sight was so awful the bile rose in her throat and she retched up her dinner onto the roots of the tree.

∽

"Look at the drowned rat!" Tessa laughed as May came in the kitchen door, the book wrapped up and hidden in her pinafore.

"Leave her alone," Mrs. Goodwin said. "Come and have some tea to warm you. Connie, pour another cup."

"No, thank you."

May hurried past and up the back stairs to Lily's bedroom. Leaning back against the closed door, she opened her pinafore and forced herself to look at the damage. The book was broken open, the spine cracked, the pages crumpled and muddy, some torn. May laid it on the floor and tried to smooth the pages out and press the book closed, but she knew it was useless. Kneeling, she slid the book, still wrapped in the pinafore, far back in the shadows under Lily's bed behind the chamber pots. Bending her head to the dusty floor, she groaned, "What should I do?" and felt the unexpected warmth of Tabbie's arm around her shoulders.

She carried the burden of what she'd done through the servants' supper, through helping Lily clean the master's wet shoes and jacket.

"What's up with you?" Lily asked, but May just shook her head. "Suit yourself, but you should consider yourself lucky, Maysie. I'd give my eye teeth for every afternoon off, and it's going to get really busy when he has people to stay this weekend."

"I'll help, I will! I don't need afternoons off, I'd rather be with you, Lil, honest."

She felt Lily's eyes on her, like she could see all the way upstairs to the tattered parcel beneath her bed.

"No need to fret. You can help us get the guest rooms spic and span tomorrow if you like, but you have to take the afternoons off. It's the Master's orders."

Oh, the Master. That man with the kind eyes like Dada's, eyes that would turn stony and worse – disappointed – when he saw what she'd done to his beautiful book, but she wouldn't shirk it, she'd own up even if it caused him to send her away. But oh, what if it cost Lily her place? The sickness in her stomach caused a cramping that sent her hurrying to the WC near the boot room.

The next morning, she polished, swept, and worked the donkey in one bedroom after another, rooms she hadn't known were there. She laid perfect fires, polished mirrors and knick-knacks, and swept rugs on her hands and knees with a brush and dustpan. In the corridor, she heard Tessa say to Lily, "That sister of yours is a hard worker, I've got to give her that."

After the midday dinner, May asked Lily if she could help her and Connie to wash and dry the special china, but Lily refused. "Just go and play. It's a lovely day out. You can help with the silver later."

As Mr. Avery pushed back his chair and went outside to smoke a cigarette, May followed him. "Is the Master home this afternoon?"

He looked down at her, amused. "What's it to you, squirt?"

"Just wondered."

He leaned back against the stonework and tucked one leg up. "He said he was going to sit in the garden. Must be nice to live a life of leisure, don't you think? Having other people do all the dirty work. That'll be me someday, I swear."

May scuffed at the gravel with her boot. Mr. Avery pursed his lips and blew out three perfect rings of smoke. He grinned down at her. "Not everyone can do that, you know."

She crept up the back stairs to fetch the book, still wrapped in the pinafore, and walked around to the back of the house. The Master was lying in a deckchair, Match and Dash at his feet. She saw the top of his panama hat over the canvas and his right hand dangling a lit cigarette just above the grass. She came cautiously around to the front of his chair and saw his eyes were closed. As the dogs lifted their heads and looked at her with their deep and sorrowful eyes, she almost ran away there and then, but the Master's eyes opened just as the tip of his cigarette touched the grass.

"Sir, look out!"

As he struggled to free himself from the deckchair, she rushed in and stomped on the smouldering patch of lawn.

"Good lord!" He looked up at her, his hand shading his eyes. "Where did you appear from? Are you my guardian angel?"

Her heart beat so hard she could feel it in her neck. "No, sir."

He settled his hat on his head and looked up at her through eyes narrowed against the sun. "Do stand a little to the left so I can see you properly."

She shuffled sideways. "Ah, that's better. So how did you happen to be here just in time, Miss May Hallam? Do I need to take you with me everywhere? I think I might."

His kind eyes, the look that Dada would give her when he teased her. She swallowed hard and held out the bundle in her arms.

"What've you got there?" he asked.

She held it closer to him, and he took it, lifting the wings of the dirty pinafore between his thumb and forefinger to reveal the broken book.

"I'm so very, very sorry, sir. It was the hunt. It startled me and I lost my grip on it. I should never have been up the tree, I know, but I'd never got a single speck on it before, but they came so fast and it just fell from under my arm and the horses..."

He looked at the book then up at her face and then down again. "This is a sorry state of affairs."

Her face flamed like the burning grass. She wanted to tell him she'd find a way to repay him for the damage, she'd clean out Benjy's stable and turn over the ash pit every day and empty slops, she'd do anything he asked, but she couldn't speak again because of the tight ball that was in her throat so she stared down at the bright green stripes of the lawn.

"The hunt, you say?"

She nodded.

"Which field?"

She pointed to the hedge.

"Oh, that tree. It's a climber all right. I used to shin up it a lot when I was a boy. There's a place that's quite perfect for reading, I remember."

She dared to look at him. He hauled himself up out of his chair and stood over her. "Well, you saved me from a fiery death so I think I can let bygones be bygones."

May couldn't trust what she was hearing. "But the book, it's ruined."

He tossed it on the deckchair, and the pinafore fell onto the grass. "So it is. Miss May Hallam, would you care to take a turn with me?"

May shot an anxious glance at the large windows overlooking the lawn. Mr. Moncrieff would be horrified if he saw her there, but the Master had set off already, hands clasped behind his back. "Tell me about your family, Miss May. How many are there in your brood? A hundred?"

She surprised herself by laughing, the relief just beginning to seep through her body. She'd been braced for his wrath, not for this gentle ribbing. "Just six, sir. And Mam."

"Father gone?"

"Dead, sir."

"Sorry to hear it," he said, stopping to smell a rose in one of the beds that bordered the lawn. He bent it towards May, and she breathed in its sweetness, still stunned by his lack of anger.

"How old are all these brothers and sisters of yours?"

"Well, it starts with Tom. He's 19, then Len, who's 17. Lily's 15, then there's a gap before Ada –"

"Your sister's only 15?"

"Yes, sir."

He tipped his hat further over his eyes. "I must say, it's jolly hard to tell with young people these days. Does she have a sweetheart, your sister?"

May was startled. "No! Mam would never hear of it."

"Ah, but what if Mam didn't know? What if she were walking out with someone here, a nice young man from Ringhampton, say?"

May thought of the distaste on Lily's face whenever Tessa talked about her suitor in Brighton. "No, not Lily. She wouldn't."

He opened his cigarette case, offering it to May with a bow. She shook her head with a smile.

"I'm perfectly sure you're right," he said, tapping a cigarette on the outside of the case, "Forgive all the questions. I can't help but be curious about the people who live under my roof."

As he paused to light his cigarette, it occurred to May that he must be lonely, having no wife or friend to talk to and keep him company. And she wondered if he had a Tabbie to talk to in his head or even out loud in bed after Mr. Avery had settled him in for the night.

They walked on side by side under the hot sun, and then all at once he stopped in his tracks and swung around to face her. "We'll say no more about the book, eh? It was just an accident, could have happened to the best of us."

At last, she allowed herself to feel the full glow of her relief. "Thank you very, very much, sir."

"What did you make of the story?"

She pressed her lips together. "I wasn't finished, sir, but I liked it very much."

He bent his knees to look her square in the face. "Come now, what about all those beatings and other dreadful things?"

"Oh no, sir, that's not what I meant. What I liked was that it told us how the horses really feel about how people treat them. And how they're all different, their characters and their bodies."

He laughed. "You're going to be a veterinarian one day, Miss May Hallam, or I'll eat my hat."

The weekend was a blur of people running this way and that, the jangle of bells, the sounds of laughter and women's voices floating through the house. Tessa and Lily did double duty as ladies' maids and servers of dinner. May saw by the set of Lily's mouth how much she felt the strain of it. May was put to work in the kitchen, kneading dough, chopping vegetables, helping to unload the sweet-smelling laundry in wicker baskets. Even Mr. Moncrieff asked for her assistance as he laid the elegant table in the dining room, both of them wearing white gloves so they wouldn't mark the gleaming silver.

After dinner was cleared away, Lily and Tessa were able to sit down and rest their feet for a few moments before going up to prepare the beds and help the lady guests to undress.

"What was it like?" May asked Lily, thinking of how the dining room must have looked full of men in black and white and the ladies in colourful summer dresses.

"I barely noticed. I was too busy trying not to trip or spill anything. My hands would keep trembling."

Mr. Moncrieff came into the kitchen and asked for their attention. "Someone has telephoned the master from Brighton to say a zeppelin has been spotted."

"No!"

"Here?"

Mrs. Goodwin shuddered. "All these flying machines. It's going to end badly if you ask me."

Mr. Moncrieff raised an eyebrow. "Perhaps you're right, but what I came to tell you is that Mr. Birmingham has given permission for everyone to come out on the lawn to see it. Yes Connie, even you."

After they'd tidied their hair and put on clean aprons, Mr. Moncrieff led the way outside. The ladies and gentlemen were already out on the lawn, staring up at the overcast sky that was fading into night. Mr. Birmingham glanced in their direction. May raised a hand to wave, but Lily grabbed her arm.

"What are you playing at?"

"He's my friend."

"He is no such thing."

Tessa nudged her. "Pay attention, silly, or you'll miss it."

May looked up, shielding her eyes from the light from the open French windows. There were different layers of darkness like overlapping curtains, some denser than others, and behind the shifting layers, May caught glimpses of a glassy, star-pocked sky. She heard a lady guest say, "How exciting it would be to see one! The Times said that they've been taking civilian passengers on the test flights. I still can't see anything, can you?"

Just as she stopped speaking, someone shouted, "Look!" and a long slim shadow moved out from behind a cloud and stole very slowly across the open sky, sliding out of sight behind another cloud.

"How can there be *people* up there in that thing?" Tessa whispered.

They stood a while longer, looking upwards, but the mysterious shape in the sky did not reappear.

"I've read they can fly up to heights of 10,000 feet. Absolutely remarkable, isn't it?" May heard a gentleman say and felt dizzy. What could it be like to look down from that high, knowing there was nothing but emptiness between you and the ground?

"I don't find it comforting to know the Germans can watch us from a great height," observed a lady guest.

"No, of course not," the gentleman replied, "I wish one of our own chaps had invented the thing. But it is a magnificent feat of engineering, you must admit."

May saw Mr. Birmingham blow his cigar smoke into the night air and grimace. "Progress isn't always a good thing, old chap."

As he turned to go back in through the French windows, he glanced towards where May was standing, but she saw that he was gazing not at her but at Lily and Tessa, who were still peering upwards at the sky with their hands cupped around their eyes. As the others drifted back into the house, May lingered on the lawn for one more look up at the mysterious clouds, breathing in the smell of cut grass and holding Tabbie's hand in hers.

On the morning Mr. Birmingham was due to leave for the Test Match in London, he called Lily and May into the library. They found him by the open window, wearing a brightly striped blazer and poking at a pipe with a penknife. "I hear you ladies will be off before I get back. I wanted to bid you farewell."

Lily curtseyed her thanks.

"Will you be sorry to leave us, Miss May Hallam?"

"Yes sir. Thank you for letting me stay here."

"Well, it's all very well, but I'm not sure I can do without you. I don't suppose you could come back with Miss Lily here after you've had your little holiday, hm?"

May smiled and shifted from foot to foot. She knew he was joking, but didn't know how to reply. Mr. Birmingham continued to poke at his pipe but glanced up. "What do you think of that, Miss Lily?"

"We're most grateful sir, but May has to go back to school after haymaking."

"Oh dear, school. I believe we have a school here in the village. Couldn't she go to that one?"

May began to wonder if he was joking after all. "But sir, I really can't stay away any longer. Davey can't do without me."

Mr. Birmingham picked up his tobacco pouch and began stuffing the brown thready stuff into the pipe bowl.

"Oh dear, is Davey your sweetheart?"

May laughed out loud and even Lily smiled. "No sir. Davey is my – our brother."

"Is he a little 'un?"

Lily and May glanced at each other.

"Sort of," May said. Hadn't she told him before about her brothers and sisters? Perhaps he hadn't listened very closely.

Mr. Birmingham considered the two girls as he tamped the tobacco into his pipe. "Well, I suppose I'll have to resign myself to losing you, young May. But you, Miss Lily, you'll be coming back after haymaking, will you not?"

"Yes sir. I hope so, sir. If you'll have me."

His eyes rested on Lily for quite a time before he replied. May glanced up at her sister and saw a flush slowly mount up her face from the neck. "Oh yes. I'll have you. Are you happy here?"

"Thank you, sir, yes. It's a very good place."

"Not too much work?"

Lily hesitated. "Just the right amount, sir."

He laughed. "A diplomatic answer if ever I heard one."

He crossed the room and picked up a book from a tall table behind the leather sofa. "Here, Miss May, a present to remember your old friend by."

It was another *Black Beauty* in the same beautiful blue binding with the title in golden letters, not a spot of mud on its pages, no hoofmarks on its spine. May couldn't find her voice.

"Thank you, sir," Lily said, leaning over to look at it. "That's very kind of you."

May looked up at him. "It's mine? To keep?"

"Yes, you noodle, to keep. Now off you go, both of you." He put the pipe in his mouth and turned to reach for his matches but then paused. "No wait, we should shake."

May put out her hand. He took it in his own large, smooth hand and pumped it up and down twice. "It's been a pleasure, Miss May. Come again."

"Thank you very much for the book."

"Think nothing of it."

And he held out his hand to Lily, who took it, looking down at the floor. "Come back to us soon, Miss Liliana."

She nodded, her face flaming, and as he turned away to light his pipe, she gripped May by the wrist, and they slipped out of the door. Lily closed it carefully behind them. In the corridor, she leaned back against the wall, her face shiny with sweat. "He makes me so nervous. I never know what he's going to say."

May was looking at the book. "Look Lil, look what he wrote."

In the flyleaf in a tight but elegant hand, he had written:

To Miss May who saved the day – and the pony. I am forever in your debt.

Walter Birmingham.

After Mr. Avery had driven the master off to the station, the whole house seemed to sag with a weary relief. Mr. Moncrieff filled his pipe and got out his stamp collection, and the women carried the heavy picnic basket between them to Ringhampton, where they took a bus to the beach at Hove. And at last May came face to face with the blue triangle in the fold of the downs, which turned out to be a loud, churning monster that crashed against the rocks and burst upwards into seethes of spray. The wind blew her hair in her face, and grains of sand lodged in the curve of her ears.

"Get your boots off, girls!" Tessa shouted above the wind. "Let's go for a paddle!"

May held Lily's hand very tightly as they staggered towards the churn and foam, the shingle hard on their bare feet. Lily and Tessa ran in up to their knees, but May refused to go beyond the furthest edge of the spreading waves where the flat wet sand oozed with frothy bubbles, like tiny creatures were drowning. The wet sand grasped her round the ankles, rooting her, claiming her for the sea.

In a panic, she pulled her feet up one by one with a schlooping sound and ran back up the beach, the shingle warm and slippery but reassuringly firm under her feet.

"It's a fine day," Mrs. Goodwin said, leaning back on her bare mottled arms, her face turned up to the sun. Connie unpacked the basket, laying out bottles of ginger beer, sandwiches, and Cornish pasties wrapped in waxed paper. Lily and Tessa came back and threw themselves on the blanket, panting and laughing.

"Are we eating already?" May asked. Tessa, lying on her back with her hands folded over her waist, answered with her eyes closed, "Why not? That's what we're here for, ain't it?"

It was hard to get comfortable on the stones, and everything May ate tasted of salt. The waves curled and plunged towards the shore and foamed up over the shingle towards them, pulling back just in time, sucking at the stones. At the end of the beach, wet rocks gleamed black, patched with emerald slime. Fishing boats rode the horizon, followed by great clouds of seabirds.

"They'll be after the fish," Mrs. Goodwin said, her mouth full of pastie. "The men throw the leavings over the side."

Gulls stalked around the edge of their blanket. Tessa threw scraps of crust, and the gulls dived to catch them, clashing and scrabbling, wheeling away, shrieking, their white wings flailing. The cruel curve of their beaks as they stabbed at the crusts made May keep her head down low, her hands over her ears. When the girls went down to the water again, May stayed behind, taking slow bites of an egg sandwich.

"Are you looking forward to going home, May?" Mrs. Goodwin asked her.

"Very much. But I liked it here. I thought I wouldn't."

"Why's that then?"

"Because I had to leave important things behind, mostly my brother."

"Is that the feeble-minded boy?"

"Yes, Davey. I have other brothers, but he's the one who's mine."

"You mean to take care of?"

"Yes."

"He'll have missed you then."

May couldn't find the words to answer so just kept on pushing a stick down between the shingle, trying to reach the sand underneath.

"I expect he's had a grand old time. Just think of all you'll have to tell him."

It was funny how kindness was sometimes so much harder to bear than the opposite. And then Lily, Tessa, and Connie came running back up the beach, screaming with laughter. An unexpected wave had drenched Connie from head to toe. Mrs. Goodwin hauled herself to her feet. "You silly beggars. It's just as well I brought a towel."

CHAPTER 14

TUESDAY, AUGUST 4 1914

May and Davey carried one of the baskets between them, with Mam and Ada coming up behind with the other. The handles dug into May's palm, and she had to throw her other arm out sideways to keep her balance, but Davey carried his side like it weighed nothing at all. In the weeks she'd been gone, he'd grown stronger. Sweat slid down May's neck, but a sweet breeze met them at the top of the hill, and there was shade under the trees where the barrels of cider from the Hall were set up against the hedge. The families were gathering, setting out the midday dinner. Across the field, the steam thresher, belching smoke, ground to a halt, and suddenly there was birdsong again.

The haymakers straightened their backs and put down their rakes and pitchforks. Slowly they came across the stubble, Tom and Len among them in their britches and Lily too in a white bonnet, arms red from the sun. They threw themselves on the ground, smelling of chaff and the iron tang of sweat, and took long swallows from the cups of ginger beer Mam handed them without a word.

May pushed down her stockings to feel the breeze on her legs and reached into the basket for torn-off pieces of Mam's cottage loaf and bacon slices for her and Davey.

Tom ragged them. "Don't know why you two are so hungry. You've done nowt all morning."

May threw a pickled onion at him, but he dodged and it rolled off into the grass.

"Davey, don't eat that," Mam called as she saw him stir towards it. "And close your mouth when you're chewing."

Len leaned back on one arm and bit into an apple. Mam reached over to smooth a lock of hair off his forehead, and he ducked away from her hand like it was a wasp.

Lily laughed, "You can't do that with Daisy Coulter watching, Mam."

Further down the hedge, the Coulters sat in a half-circle sharing a large pork pie, and beyond them the Irishmen sat together, the men who came over the sea to work on the harvest every year. May had helped to stuff straw into bags for them to sleep on in the barn. Their voices were rough and strange to her, and she'd seen how they looked at Mam pushing back a wisp of hair, their eyes full of some kind of longing.

A sudden breeze riffled across the field and lifted the floppy edge of Lily's bonnet. May poked her with her foot. "What would Mr. Moncrieff say if he saw you now?"

"He'd say I'll never make a ladies' maid." Lily laughed, showing the perfect white of her top teeth, and May realised her sister was pretty and that she'd probably marry soon. Probably someone who was right now watching her over the rim of his mug of cider.

She was different at home than how she was at the Grange, her whole body loose and graceful. The scuttle and hunch of her was gone, left behind like a different Lily altogether. Just a week after they'd left Sussex, it was hard to remember Mr. Birmingham with his linen jacket and cool white hat, lighting a cigarette with his long pale fingers as he looked over the sea, or Mrs. Goodwin's gap-toothed smile and floury arms. Or Tessa and her wild hair and lazy ways. None of them seemed real anymore. And Tabbie had faded now that Davey was back to being May's shadow. She needn't have worried that Ada would take her place. As soon as he saw May walk into the cottage, he became frantic, gripping her so hard around her neck that it took both Tom and Len to prise him off. He was still so nervous she'd leave him again that he sat by the outhouse door whenever she went in to do her business.

All along the hedge, men began to stand up, stiffly, stretching their backs. Tom got to his feet, slapping his hat against his thigh to shake off the hay dust. Davey sneezed and when he lifted his head, a long trail of snot dropped to the ground. Mam grabbed his nose with her handkerchief. "Blow," she commanded.

Tom looked up at the sky and spoke to Len, "Looks like the weather's staying fair. Time to load the top pasture."

The rhythms of how the Irish labourers spoke had crept into his voice. The thresher started up again, with a cough of black smoke that drifted over to the hedge. Mam stoppered up the ginger beer bottle, and she and Ada began putting things into the baskets.

"You ready, squirts?" Tom asked, and May jumped to her feet and beckoned to Davey.

They ran and jumped alongside Tom and Len on the way back down to the stable yard, pelting each other with the leavings. In the yard, Len let them lead out Birdie and Raven and hold their heads while he slipped on the big collars and harness and buckled all the many straps. Birdie stood patient and grave, but Raven threw his head up to shake off the flies, yanking at May's arm. The waggon was wheeled out with its big-spoked red wheels, spindle sides, and curved middle like a ship. The shafts were slotted into the harness, and after more buckling, Len helped them up, first May, then Davey onto the wide planked bed.

As Tom flicked the reins and the rig lurched out of the yard and started up the track, joy pulsed through May's whole body as she stood high at the front with her brothers, like four kings at the head of an army, the breeze lifting their hair. Tom clicked the horses on, and Len held Davey's waistband to keep him balanced as they rumbled up the track to the top end of the farm.

As they turned into the field, Tom called "Hold on tight." The waggon pitched and bumped over the stubble and ruts to the centre of the field where men and women were forking the haycocks together. Len jumped down first and put up a steadying hand to help May down, but Tom urged her to leap into an unraked pile of hay. Davey went first with a cry of delight and bounced right up again. When May took a flying leap, she landed in a funny way on her arm but pretended nothing had happened, just giving it a rub when no one was looking.

Mr. Kilkenny was in the field, in gaiters and shirt sleeves, twisting stalks of hay in his fingers.

"What d'you think, Tom Hallam?" he called. Tom picked up some stalks of his own and bent and twisted them, holding them to his nose.

"Crisp. And a good colour. Now we just need the weather to hold, sir."

"We do. Now let's get this lot back to the barn quick as you can."

Tom made May and Davey stay clear as the men speared the haycocks and swung them up onto the waggon to Len, who piled them close together. A rank underarm smell leeched into the sweet smell of the cut grass. May and Davey kicked a stone around and turned cartwheels in the prickly shorn grass before Mr. Kilkenny sent them to glean for loose hay to use in Mam's garden. As they gathered the stray stalks, May heard a lark trilling high above them like it was talking to itself. The stubble pricked her hands, and as she gleaned, she came upon a bloody mess that she poked with a stick and saw was a flattened, beheaded rabbit. Davey let out a cry of disgust and put his hands over his ears as May hooked it on the stick and carried it to the edge of the field to throw it in the ditch.

When the waggon was so full it looked like it would topple, the men threw ropes over the load to hold it steady, and Mr.

Kilkenny gave the signal to start back to the yard. With Tom and Len leading them, the horses strained forward, the sinews in their necks standing out, with four men on either side of the waggon holding the ropes taut.

Suddenly May remembered Black Beauty. What if this was too hard for Birdie and Raven? What if they knew this would break their knees and damage their bones, but they had no language to say so? And then she saw how her brothers gentled them along – "Come on, Birdie, that's my girl" – and gave them moments to rest and stretch their necks and had a sudden memory of her father, his muscled arms cradling a horse's head as it rested on his shoulder.

As the afternoon waned, Lily came to find them and they walked home together through the village as the shadows grew longer. The rooks called from the tops of the elms in the churchyard, and the dark yew tree loomed wide over the gate. Over the hedge came the sound of the vicar's carriage horse cropping grass and snorting. When they walked into the kitchen, Mam sent them straight back outside, pressing a sliver of soap into May's hand. "You two are filthy. Off to the pump and wash yourselves. And do it properly. Hands, face, and neck."

The cold water made May gasp, but felt good. She took some in her mouth and swallowed, leaving the taste of metal in her mouth. The dirt peeled off her face like a second skin. She helped Davey to lather up the soap between his hands, which made him giggle. They dripped into the kitchen, and Ada flung them a towel. "I hope you two wiped your boots – I just washed that floor."

Mam put plates of cabbage and potatoes in front of them. May was hungry and tucked in, but Davey's head began to sway over his plate after a few bites, his eyes closing. Mam nodded to Lily, who knelt to unlace his boots and pushed him in front of her up the stairs.

"Are Tom and Len at the Dragon?" May asked as she wiped her plate dry with a heel of bread.

"They are," Mam said, taking her plate to wash it in the scullery.

May slid off the chair and went out into the yard to wait for them. In the dusk, bats whirled around the roof. May leaned on the gate, wondering why her arm ached and then remembering the leap from the waggon. The hinges squeaked under her weight, a familiar sound, one she'd heard all her life. She was glad to be home, glad they were all home. She wondered which boy Lily would marry, maybe George Coulter from next door or awkward Sam Laidlaw from the stables.

But what if one of the Irishmen were to woo her? Sussex was far, but Ireland was even further, and there was a sea to be crossed to get there. She thought of how the waves at Hove had churned and roared, and she said a prayer that she might never have to ride across it in a boat.

She heard the jangling of a bit, and Mr. Kilkenny drove up in a pony cart, moths hurling themselves at the trap lamps. "Is your mother at home?"

There was no friendliness, no give or softness in his manner.

"She is." May opened the gate, and hearing the creak, Mam came to the door, wiping her hands on her apron, a frill of white dust around the hem of her dress. "Evening, Mr. Kilkenny. Is everything all right?"

He jumped down from the driver's seat and with one swift movement of his hand looped the reins around the gatepost. "In a manner of speaking, Mrs. Hallam. But I wanted to be the first to warn you. According to his lordship's wireless, our country is now on a war footing with Germany."

Mam's hand went to her mouth. "Oh dear, no."

Mr. Kilkenny came in through the open gate, brushing past May, and went straight to Mam. "Don't be alarmed for your boys. There'll be no need at all for them to go. I've already talked to his lordship on the telephone, and he's confident farm workers will be exempted from service. Please don't worry. I came here immediately to put your mind at ease."

He leaned in close to look at her face, and Mam turned her head away from him as if his breath was not to her liking.

"Surely all young men will be needed to fight?" she said.

"Not at all. Someone will need to feed the people left at home. Farmers do an essential job of work, Mrs. Hallam."

"Of course, I'd be grateful for my sons to be spared, but they must do their part for the country."

Over Mr. Kilkenny's shoulder, a fat three-quarter moon had risen over Granny Maitland's house. As May stroked the pony's nose, she caught the sound of voices coming from the village and turned to see if Mam had noticed. The voices grew louder, and there were shouts of laughter and the occasional burst of song. May could distinguish Tom's tenor and George Coulter's deeper bass.

Mr. Kilkenny's face took on an indulgent look. "I don't expect they've heard the news or they'd be a mite more subdued."

Mam frowned. "It's haymaking time, Mr. Kilkenny. They work hard and deserve a little fun when the day's over."

Then the boys were at the gate, their faces flushed on top of their sun-reddened skin. "Mam! Have you heard? There's going to be a war."

Mr. Kilkenny had turned to look at them. Behind his back, Mam's finger went up to her mouth to shush them. There was something bold in Tom's eye, something that made May hold in her breath and press her face against the pony's neck.

"Will you be going for a soldier, Mr. Kilkenny?" he asked.

The agent smiled as if he'd been expecting the question. "No, Tom, I'll be needed here. The country will need farmers more than ever to feed the troops. You boys will be needed here too, don't you worry."

Tom looked the agent up and down, his chest out. Mam glared at him, but he wasn't to be stopped. "Needed? I don't call it manly to shirk your patriotic duty, do you, Mr. Kilkenny?"

Mam tsked loudly and turned to Mr. Kilkenny. "Please forgive him. He's had a drop too much beer tonight."

Mr. Kilkenny began a sorrowful shake of his head. "I hope you haven't gone and done anything foolish, boys."

At this, George Coulter started moving down the lane towards his own house in an exaggerated tiptoe. Tom stood with his legs apart. "What's foolish about fighting for your country?"

Len said, "Mam, we came to tell you. There was a recruiter at the Dragon, and we all signed our names."

Tom interrupted, "For the 1st Nottinghamshire Regiment. All the boys from around here signed up – Len and me and George and Fred Arkwright and Sam Laidlaw. We'll be in it together."

As the light faded from the summer sky, May watched from behind the pony's neck. Mam looked down at the ground. "Oh boys."

Mr. Kilkenny tapped his foot, and May saw his knuckles whiten on the hand that held the whip. "So, I'm to lose two good waggoners and half of my stable staff to the Army?"

"Yes, sir, that's correct," Tom said.

"Do you realise that you've also lost your mother her home?"

Tom's mouth dropped open. "You would do that?" he asked.

"It's a tied cottage, my boy. If you don't work for the estate, his Lordship can't be expected to give your family a roof over their heads now, can he?"

There was a long silence. Len turned away and leaned on the gate, his hand on his forehead. May held her breath. Then Mam spoke. "Might there be work for me, Mr. Kilkenny? In the laundry for instance. Or maybe the dairy?"

He gave her a long look that made May feel awkward, but Mam stood quietly, the light from the open doorway across her boots, and let him stare.

"I'm sorry you should be put to that by your sons' impulsiveness, Mrs. Hallam. Understandable in the heat of the moment but not a well-thought-out decision. Perhaps if I were to have a word with the recruiting officer?"

"No," she said, putting up a hand, "If my boys believe they should fight, I won't stand in their way."

Len's head came up, and he looked at Mam like he had never really seen her before. May saw what it cost Mam to say this in the way her hands clenched and from the sag of her face that had looked so young just hours before. Tom's face cracked into a smile. "That's the way, Mam."

"You, be quiet. Boys, go and wash in the scullery. There's no more dinner, but there's bread and cheese left over and dripping in the pot."

Tom and Len edged through the open gate past where Mr. Kilkenny stood, Len looking at the ground. Tom kept his eyes on the agent's till he'd crossed the threshold. May felt the pony's hot breath against her ear and didn't dare to move. Mam reached forward to touch the agent's sleeve. "You wouldn't turn us out, Mr. Kilkenny. I'm a strong woman, I can do a good day's work for you."

He looked down at her hand on his arm. "But how will you manage here?"

"My girls are old enough to do what's needed. Even my son Davey can pump water and scrub floors. We'll manage. Please don't send us away because my sons must do their duty."

A silence rose in the moonlit yard. The hens scratched and bickered in the henhouse, and a dog barked far across the fields. Mr. Kilkenny laid his hand on top of Mam's. "Let me see what can be done."

They stood like that for a few seconds and then he turned and climbed up into the trap and tapping the pony's rump with the whip, trotted away. Mam looked over to where May still stood on the road. "He'll do right by us, Maysie, you'll see. You should be proud of your brothers."

CHAPTER 15

FEBRUARY 1915

As May and Davey were feeding potato peelings to Mrs. Coulter's pig, their breath clouding in the wintry air, they heard the tick tick of Mam's bicycle along the lane. May pulled the bucket off the lean-to and came into the yard just as Ada stepped outside to bang the kitchen mats into a haze of dust right in Mam's face.

"Did that really want doing the minute I got here?"

Mam sounded like she'd had a hard morning. She leaned the cycle against the wall and brushed off her coat. Ada scowled. "I've been scraping the floor all this long while and never a hand's help from these two."

Mam went indoors without answering. May followed, Davey at her heels, Ada pushing past them to put the rugs back in place. The washing hung on the fireguard, smelling of singe and starch. Her coat still on, Mam pulled off her mittens and sorted through the letters on the table, slitting one open and angling the paper to read it by the faint light coming from the window. It was a bleak afternoon, but they had to save lamp oil. May shushed Davey and crossed her fingers tightly in her apron pocket as Mam read the squared French paper with the censor's black marks, then folded it up and put it by.

"Are the boys going on all right?" May asked, seeing the creases in Mam's forehead grow deeper.

"Len seems the same. Says they're still on transport taking care of the horses."

The relief flooded down May's arms to the tips of her fingers. She dreaded each letter in case of bad news, and the relief only lasted as long as it took the postman to bring the next. Not that she would dream of letting anyone see how anxious she felt.

Mam slit open a letter from Lily, pulled out some banknotes and held them out to May. "Put these away for me, love?"

As she reached for the caddy, May remembered the money Mr. Kilkenny had given her and Davey that morning for pulling thistles out of the bottom field. He'd said, "Here's a shilling. It's not for you, it's for your mother. Make sure you give it to her with my compliments," but she dropped it in the caddy along with Lily's notes without saying anything about it. Mam looked up from the letter. "Lily was worried about her place, but now the other maid's gone off to do munitions work so it's just her and the cook."

How different the Grange must be now with Mr. Birmingham off with his regiment, its furniture covered in dust sheets, Match and Dash gone who knows where, and Lily and Mrs. Goodwin cosy round the kitchen table, able to go outdoors whenever their work was done.

"How was the laundry today, Mam?" she asked.

Mam sighed. "You'd think with all those machines it would be easier, but there's such a lot of sheets all the time and you wouldn't want to know what state most of them are in. Not the family of course – I mean the patients. I know the poor fellows can't help themselves, but it's a trial."

Ada dumped the darning basket on the table and pulled out a chair. "Do you ever see them? You know, the soldiers with no legs?"

Mam gave her a sharp look. "As if I have time. As if they'd let a skivvy go upstairs and see those poor souls lying under those suits of armour and fancy paintings."

Davey pressed up close to Mam's shoulder. "Why don't they have legs, Mam, those men?"

Mam patted his shoulder. "Because they were injured in France, and they're up at the big house to get better. Now don't carry on, they're just the unlucky ones. Our Len and Tom are right as rain. Didn't we just get a letter?" And May saw her give Ada another look for putting ideas in Davey's mind.

"What about the family? Do you ever see them?" May asked.

She still had a wistful memory of the prizegiving when she'd been too shy to look up into the dazzle of Lady Sherwood's face.

"Never see hide nor hair of them. You've no idea how big that place is till you've been in it. My world in the laundry's a long way away from theirs."

Thinking about a house so enormous that it contained different worlds, May fed some sticks into the range.

"Maysie! Not so free with the kindling, if you please. If you want to be helpful, you and Davey can go out and find us more. Only fallen branches, mind. I wouldn't like to have Mr. Kilkenny accusing us of stealing."

"Can I go along, Mam?" Ada asked, "I haven't been outside this whole week."

Mam paused and glanced at the darning basket. May clenched her hands and hoped but saw that Mam was going to relent.

"I suppose, since it's my half day. But I'd thank you to be back sharpish, all of you."

Without waiting for Ada to put on her outdoor things, May dashed out with Davey on her heels and set off down the road. She heard Ada behind her, running to catch up, still struggling to put her arms in the sleeves of her coat. The day held the kind of cold that finds a way in the space between the cuff and the glove, the scarf and the collar, the kind of sodden cold that doesn't brighten the cheeks but makes the nose run. Davey poked May and spoke in her ear so loud that Ada couldn't fail to hear. "Shall we show Ada the fairy grotto?"

May turned and saw Ada's lip start to curl. "I don't see why we should. She'd only spoil it."

Ada stopped walking. "I don't even know what it is. And maybe I don't care."

May felt her face turning red. "I should like to know why we'd ever want to share it with you."

Ada's face twisted into a full-blown sneer. "You and your stupid fairy house. That's just like you – always playing instead of working. Davey can't help it, the big booby, but you're just a lazy madam."

The unfairness of it when they'd spent all morning dragging those thistles out of the field. "You take that back."

"I won't."

"Well, go home then. We don't want you." And she gave Ada a good hard shove in the chest, feeling the roughness of her jersey on her bare hands. Ada staggered back a step but held her ground, a strange look on her face. May stood with her legs apart, eyes locked on hers till Ada gave her head a little shake and, with a last murmur of contempt, turned and tramped back down the road.

"Good riddance," May shouted to her sister's retreating back.

Davey did a dance, kicking up leaves and singing, "We don't want old Ada, no, we don't."

May walked on towards the wood, with Davey skipping beside her, dodging puddles of murky green water. She felt the squeeze in her chest slowly ease as she moved, swinging her arms to stay warm. The hedgerow was a tangle of dead-looking brambles, and she picked some leftover blackberries to share with Davey, pips lodging between her teeth. They stopped to look into the ditch where a brackish stream flowed over a fretwork of old dead leaves. As the sun forced its way through the silver sheen of the sky, greys and muddy browns lit up and became green and terracotta. The still-silver sky grew bluer, only to fade back into grey as the clouds thickened.

The feathered edge of the bare trees on the skyline looked as soft as fur. May lifted her hand and stroked their distant silhouettes like the spine of a cat. All she could hear was the trilling of a thrush and a distant whinny from the direction of the stables, and the hard stone and brick of a city like London seemed an impossibility, a place she'd moved through in a dream, knowing it was a dream even as she slept.

They left the road and climbed a stile into a field of trampled grass with blackened patches where gypsies had built their fires. Davey picked up a charred stick and promptly dropped it. "It's warm!"

"They can't have been gone long. We must have just missed them."

Wheel tracks were sunk in the muddy ground, pitted with horseshoe marks, dung ground into the ruts. Davey stepped in a pile of it, and May helped him to scrape it off his boot on the grass.

Inside the wood, the trees were close and bare, the ground a tangle of foliage and bindweed. A magpie flashed from tree to tree. They passed an upended tree stump, clods of clay clinging to its root ball, and some cold-looking snowdrops poked through the mulched-down leaves around it.

"Look," she said, pointing at a large hare lolloping away from the sound of their boots in the understory. Davey laughed and then turned to her in dismay. "What if there's a trap, Maysie?"

She shook her head. "The poachers won't have been out in this cold weather."

Lying to Davey was as smooth as pouring cream from the top of the jug. He trusted her completely, and she used it to her advantage. Otherwise, he'd only fret and pester till her patience was tested.

The trees grew denser, and May knew they must be getting near the place. On a mellow autumn day when the war was still a new thing that she didn't quite believe in, she and Davey had hollowed out some spaces in the clay bank and made rooms for imaginary tiny people. They had to search around to find it, over-grown and almost hidden from sight, but it was still there. Davey whooped and cantered about the clearing as May scooped out the dry leaves that had lodged in the hollows.

"We can make it a house again. Let's find some moss for carpets."

They carefully peeled bright green patches off boulders, and May pressed them into place on the floor of the clay rooms. From her pocket, she brought out the odd buttons, empty cotton reels, and fabric scraps she had rescued from the sewing box to furnish the hollows.

"Look, Maysie!" Davey tipped into her hands an empty snail shell, a dainty grey feather tipped in brown, and best of all, the tiny skull of a bird.

"What good finds! We can use them all in the parlour."

Davey reached his hand to touch her careful arrangement, but she pushed him away.

"Don't! You'll spoil it. Go and find more things. What about some dandelion heads for the walls? Not the clocks, the yellow ones. If you can find any – it might be too cold."

Davey sighed and shuffled off through the leaves.

There were no people in the clay bank house, but May pretended they were there, a father smelling of pipe smoke. And a mother who wore pretty dresses and embroidered in a chair while a maid did the plain sewing and a cook fed the range and boiled the hams. And six children, but for that she'd need to hollow out a lot more rooms. She thought of the many unused rooms at the Grange and the upstairs sitting room that Mr. Birm-ingham had furnished with such care for a wife he didn't have. All those rooms for just one man to move from one to the other as he pleased, all those wide windows in the red brick, and an attic for the many people who took care of him. Walter Birming-ham. She sat back on her heels and wondered if he was in

France, bending over to look at a spread-out map of the battlefield.

The air shifted in the stillness, and May noticed the light was fading. It would still be light outside the wood, but she and Davey should hurry and find some kindling before it was too dark to see. She heard the rustling of footsteps and, suddenly afraid, she called out, "Davey!" A startled pigeon burst out of the hedgerow, and then there was a crumpling sound. May jumped to her feet. Nothing moved in the treetops and the air was very still, and then all at once it was pierced by a long, high-pitched howl.

"Davey?"

She stumbled towards the direction of the howling, tripping on roots, fearing the brutal teeth of a trap snapped around his leg, and found him tipped forward on his hands and knees, almost swallowed up in a waist-high bed of nettles. "I'm here, Davey, I'm here." It was bad but not as bad as a trap. She tried pulling at the back of his jacket, but he wouldn't budge, howling at a higher pitch. "Davey, come on, you've got to help me." The nettles were right up against his face, which was turning a mottled purple. She plunged her arms in, gritting her teeth against the stings, and seized Davey under the armpits and pulled as hard as she could. He came loose like a stubborn thistle, and they both fell backwards, his elbow hitting her in the stomach, knocking the breath out of her. She rolled him off her, her bare hands smarting. He lay on his side, still shrieking, and she thumped him on the back.

"Shut up! It's not helping."

Startled, he drew a breath in and before he could exhale, May clamped her hand over his mouth.

"Stop it! I know it hurts, but I can make it better."

She took her hand away from his mouth and, as he whimpered, scrambled to her feet and pulled up handfuls of the dock leaves that grew along the edge of the nettle bed.

"Look, Davey, these'll help. Now sit up." She tried to act calm and stopped herself from wincing at the sight of the rising purple ridges on his face. His hands were even more raw than hers. As soon as she laid the dock leaf against the skin of his left hand, he let out a scream.

"Now come on, you've got to let me dab it, Davey. It'll help, you'll see." She pressed on, gripping his hand tighter, as he tried to pull it away. "Now the other one. Come on Davey, try to be brave."

Before she could stop him, he'd rubbed his eye with his other hand and the screaming began again. May sat back, her legs out in front of her and let him howl. Maybe someone would hear him and come to help. She looked up at the towering, leafless trees and saw how the darkness was spreading slowly downwards like a cloud. Her fingers were white with cold except for the slashes of rash on her palms, and inside her boots her chilblains ached.

When Davey's screams sank to a whimper, she tried to get him to stand up.

"We have to go home. Mam'll make it better, you'll see she will."

But there was no Mam with them in the wood, in the gathering dark. There was only May to decide what to do for the best. Starting to feel the beginnings of alarm, she tugged at Davey's arm, but he wailed and turned away from her, curling into a ball. The air was heavy with coming rain, and the only sound was the rapid tap-tap-tap of a distant woodpecker. She couldn't go to fetch help, leaving him terrified and alone in the dark, so she'd have to stay where she was, huddled against him to try to keep them both warm. She thought of making a small fire but was afraid to risk the flames and sparks. Davey's breathing had slowed and as his lips parted, she heard a shallow snore.

As the cold worked its way to her chest, she had a sudden thought of the future, of herself in her own house with a husband and children. Would Davey still be cleaved to her then? Her brain felt tight and achy as she imagined it going on forever, his need of her, over and over into the unknown future that tipped over the horizon, but then having to leave him was not to be borne either, not knowing if he was distressed or happy, not knowing if he needed her. They were two as one, halves of the same whole, and in the cold, night-calling wood, she saw that it would never not be that way.

She rubbed her temples with the heels of her hands to try to ease the ache in her head. There were no sounds except the patter of rain that she couldn't yet feel. Davey mumbled something in his sleep, and May lay down next to him, her back pressed against his. She tried to imagine Tabbie lying with her, front to front, rubbing her hands to warm them, but couldn't summon her. She must still be straddling the oak in the field behind the Grange or floating through the house as everyone slept. May bit her lip and tucked her hands under her arms and, with her knees pulled to her chest, tried to remember the words of the poem she'd recited at the summer pageant, the noble-sounding words and swelling ending, and as the words slipped and scrambled and slid away from her, she saw her father, saw his mouth move, the fear in his eyes that turned into Mr. Birmingham's green eyes and then all at once she could hear him calling her name over and over, urgently like there was a coming danger that she couldn't see. She tried to call back, and the effort woke her, and she sat up and saw lights coming towards her and shouted, "We're here!"

From between the dark trees, the hurricane lanterns came on, the face of Mr. Coulter glowing yellow and black. "You children! Your mam's been beside herself."

And then there was old Gordon from the farrier's and, surprisingly, Mr. Kilkenny, who helped May to stand when her legs wouldn't do as they were told.

"Are you all right, lass?" Mr. Coulter asked. "How's the boy?" He bent to Davey, who was crying now, half asleep and shuddering with cold.

"He fell in the nettles and wouldn't come – I tried and tried." The quiver in her voice that she tried to crush, her frozen hands shaking, her stomach gassy with relief and hunger.

"It's all right, lass, niver you worry. We'll tek you home to your mam."

Mr. Coulter and old Gordon lifted Davey between them and set off through the trees. May said she could walk, but when she tried, her feet were too numb so Mr. Kilkenny hoisted her on his back. It was strange to be so close to his whiskers and his ears and feel his rough tweed jacket under her frozen hands. The wood suddenly seemed small and safe in the light of the lamps and in the presence of the men. May could hear them breathing heavily as Davey clung around their necks.

When Mam opened the door, her face was white and set like May had never seen it before. Davey began to wail as soon as he saw her. Mrs. Coulter and Mrs. Walton crowded into the doorway, and Mrs. Coulter cried out, "Oh thank the heavens."

The men set him down in Dada's chair and stood back, wiping their brows, and Mam knelt in front of him, moaning at the state of his hands and face. She asked Mrs. Coulter to run to Granny Maitland's for clover honey to put on his nettle burns, while Mrs. Walton sat May down in a kitchen chair, wrapped her in a blanket warm from the fireguard and brought her a basin of steaming water for her stinging hands and frozen feet. The comfort of it brought tears to May's eyes, but she gritted her teeth until they passed. Mam was not in the mood to stand it.

Mam and Mrs. Coulter gently dabbed the honey on Davey's face and hands as he twisted and wailed. The men slipped away, but Mr. Kilkenny lingered, asking if he could be of further service. Mam rose from her knees and led him to the door. "I'm very grateful to you, Mr. Kilkenny. I'm mortified to have put you to such trouble."

May saw him take Mam's hand. "Who wouldn't wish to help to find a lost child? Or in this case two. I hope they'll learn a lesson from this."

"Oh, I'll make sure of that, Mr. Kilkenny."

"Perhaps I could call tomorrow to see how everyone is feeling?"

Mam's voice was so quiet in reply that May couldn't hear the words. From across the kitchen table, Ada's eyes caught hers, then slid back to her mending as she whispered, "You're going to catch it this time."

It had to come, and as soon as the door shut on Mr. Kilkenny, the candles on the mantel flickering in the draught, Mam began, her voice pitched high and loud. "How could you let Davey out of your sight? You know how he wanders off. He can't be left, you know that. How can I trust you after this? Look at the state of him!"

Hearing the anger in Mam's voice, Davey's lips puckered. "Mam, no!"

"That's enough, Davey. I'm talking to May. Look at the rash on him. If it turns out he needs a doctor, do you really think we can afford that half-crown?"

May tried to speak, "I tried dock leaves, Mam, I did, but Davey wouldn't move. He's stronger than me and I can't always –"

"I don't want to hear a word from you. I sent you out for firewood, but did you bring any? I don't see any."

May hung her head.

"You give too much thought to playing. That was all very well before the war, but now there's no time for fun. You know how I rely on you with Davey, and now you've let me down."

May bit her tongue hard till her voice was steady enough to speak. "It was only this one time, and I'm so sorry."

The kitchen was very quiet except for Davey's whimpering and the lap of water as Mrs. Walton took the basin to the scullery to pour away the water. From the other side of the lamp, Ada looked at May in undisguised delight. Mam pulled out a chair and sank onto it. "Can't you see, Maysie? I can't keep this family going without you."

May stood up, the floor cold on her thawing feet, and came to Mam, arms limp at her sides. "I'll never let you down again as long as I live, Mam. I won't. Ever."

And then she was crying into Mam's hair, and Mam was holding her and the air in the room seemed to sag and settle. Mam patted May's back and then pushed her gently away. "Now then, don't carry on so. Ada, be good enough to bring some ham and cold potatoes for May and Davey. And boil that kettle for more tea."

Food had never tasted so good, not even the servants' dinner at Warrington Grange. May held her knife and fork gingerly in her still smarting hands. Davey was allowed to stay in Dada's chair to eat, but as Mam saw him tip over into sleep, she took his plate away and tucked a shawl around him. "He'll need you to stay with him tonight, Maysie."

"Yes Mam."

"Don't speak with your mouth full."

That was for the schoolmistress's benefit, but Mrs. Walton had another concern. "Is that wise, Addie? Aren't they a little old to be sleeping together, even with Davey as he is?"

"It's quite all right, Frances. Davey sleeps in the boys' big bed and May has a cot at the foot."

May caught Mrs. Walton's eye and nodded heartily to back Mam up, though she often woke in the mornings with Davey's bulk beside her, one arm thrown across her waist.

As Ada poured the tea, Mam cut thin slices of cake for the ladies, and May knew there'd be no more cake at home for the rest of the week. She smeared the last bite of ham around her plate to catch any lingering crumbles of potato and took her plate into the scullery to rinse it clean. Coming back into the kitchen, she sat down next to Ada.

"What?"

"I'll help."

"You don't fool me. You're just looking to get back into Mam's good graces."

"Will you let me help or not?"

Ada thrust a pair of grey woollen eels at her. "Then you can have Davey's socks. The toes always want doing."

May sighed and reached into the sewing box for a thimble. As she threaded the darning needle, she heard Mrs. Coulter say quietly to Mam, "Do you know what you're going to do about the question yet?"

Mrs. Walton nodded her head in May and Ada's direction, but Mam said, "Let them listen. They should hear what a pass this family's come to."

"What pass, Mam?" May asked, with an uneasy feeling, rubbing her bare heels against the chair rung to scratch her chilblains.

"The pass is if I lose my job, we'll have nowhere to live."

Mrs. Walton shook her head. "It's going to be all right, girls. Your mother's worrying for nothing."

"It's not nothing, Frances. We can't live on what Lily sends and what the boys can spare from their army wages. Not without a roof over our heads."

It was always a surprise to hear her own mother contradict the schoolmistress.

"Why would we lose this house?" Ada asked.

"You know very well if none of us works on the estate, Lord Sherwood has no reason to give us lodging."

Ada persisted. "I know, but why would you lose your job at the laundry?"

The three women exchanged glances and Mrs. Coulter said "All the more reason to accept Mr. Kilkenny's proposal, Adeline."

May looked from one woman's face to the others. Mrs. Coulter was shaking her head in a "mark my words" way, and Mrs. Walton was frowning, the tip of her tongue between her teeth. Mam had her grim face on, and she looked tired, the creases round her eyes deeper and longer than May remembered.

"What kind of proposal?" she asked.

"A marriage proposal," Mrs. Coulter said, "He's asked your mother to marry him."

"What?" She and Ada had said it together. Mr. Kilkenny who'd been so friendly and helpful, but in a way that felt not quite straight. Who'd stared at Mam like he was looking at a horse for sale.

"You should seriously consider it, Addie," Mrs. Coulter continued, "He makes a very good wage and I'm sure he's been saving his money up. And you'd live at Home Farm and hobnob with the family at the Hall. Think of that."

Mam pulled a face. "He likes to boast about talking to his lordship, but they're not asking him to sup with them."

Mrs. Walton shook her head. "You know my feeling about it. You'll be exchanging one kind of struggle for another."

May interrupted. "Do you like him, Mam?"

"Not especially. He strikes me as a hard man to please."

Mrs. Walton put her cup and saucer on the table. "And he uses blackmail to do his wooing."

May looked at Ada. She wasn't entirely sure what blackmail was, and Ada seemed none the wiser either. Seeing their faces, Mam sighed. "If I don't marry him, he'll make sure I'm dismissed from the laundry, and we'll lose our home."

Mrs. Coulter looked surprised. "He said that very thing?"

"No, but he made a very strong hint. It wasn't an offer made to please."

Mrs. Walton put her cup down and pushed it aside, putting both hands flat on the table. "Let's think about your alternatives, Addie. You could tell his lordship about Mr. Kilkenny's threat."

"And who's he going to believe, his agent or some ragtag in the laundry?"

"You're not ragtag, you're Cyril Hallam's wife, and your sons are serving their country."

Scratching spots of wax off the table with her thumbnail, May tried to imagine Mam in a stiff silk dress on Mr. Kilkenny's arm at church, the six of them walking behind. Her neck went hot. "Tom won't like it," she couldn't help saying.

Mam sighed. "I've said I can't give him an answer with the boys away."

"But what if he asks again?" May asked.

"Never you mind that."

The room was growing cooler, but May knew better than to

offer to stoke the range. Her bare feet were raw and cold, the chilblains stabbing like needles.

Mrs. Walton asked "Hasn't your sister-in-law offered to have you all?"

Mam shook her head. "She has. She's a good woman, but she has her own way of doing things. I wouldn't be mistress in my own home."

"Perhaps if you got a job, maybe in one of the factories, you could save up for a house for you and the children," Mrs. Walton suggested.

Mrs. Coulter pulled a face. "I shouldn't like that meself, being cooped up indoors all day, would you, Addie? Give me the fresh air."

Mrs. Walton persisted. "They're paying good wages at the munitions factories, even to the women."

May saw that Mam didn't like the way the schoolmistress wouldn't leave the subject be. "I don't think I've got the strength for a job like that."

"Heavens, Addie, I've seen you beat carpets and lift a heavy copper like it was nothing."

Mam sighed. "I have Davey to think of. It'd be too much of a wrench for him, leaving."

May watched her teacher's face, the way it softened and hardened at the same time. Mrs. Walton pushed back her chair and stood up. "I dare say, but if you give in and marry that man, you'll like as not be his drudge till kingdom come. He'll not treat you well, I know his type."

She took her mackintosh from the pegs by the door and pulled her arms through the sleeves. Resting a hand on Mam's shoulder she said, "Addie dear, don't let pride stop you from doing what's best. Better to be beholden to your sister-in-law than to that man."

Mam sighed and stood up. "I'll think on it some more, Frances. I can promise you that."

As May dipped the darning needle in and out of the ragged edges of the sock, she listened to the rain splattering the window and imagined the cottage as it would look if they were gone, the range cold and dead, the slow drip of the pump in the scullery. When Mam came back from seeing the teacher out, Mrs. Coulter also rose. "I'll be getting along myself. I'm so thankful these two are safe and sound."

Mam looked at Davey, her face soft and slack. "Thanks for your all help, Carrie."

"It's nothing to mention."

"Have you an umbrella?"

"It's just a step," she said, wrapping her shawl around her, "Good evening to you all."

Mam locked the door behind her and came to gather the teacups and cake plates to wash. "Come along you two, Davey wants taking up to bed. Can I trust you two to do it? Careful now, he's all over honey."

With one of his sticky arms over each of their shoulders, May and Ada pushed and dragged Davey, still more than half asleep, up the stairs and laid him on the wide bed in the boys' room. Ada straightened up, her hand in the small of her back.

"You deal with him. I've got the range to bank up and the wood to stack."

"Please yourself," May said, toeing the door closed behind her. She turned Davey over on his side and tucked the blankets around him. He was already asleep again, his breath coming thick and steady. The room smelled damp, and she could feel a draught through the crack in the window glass. About to rattle the curtains shut, she paused to listen to the rain turning the yard to mud. They could still be out there, she and Davey, in that bitter, drenching darkness. Undoing her clothes, she lay down in her underthings on the bolster on the floor, too tired to fetch her nightdress from the other room. Her eyes dragged shut as the blankets began to warm her, but she forced them open, and staring up at the knotted boards of the ceiling, said a prayer of thanks to Dada and Mr. Birmingham for coming to their rescue.

CHAPTER 16

EARLY OCTOBER 1915

The moon in its white coatshell rode just above the sill of the open window. May couldn't say what time it was. The sky was a hazy blue above the trees, but the garden below was already dark. She sat on the clothes chest watching Ada to make sure she was asleep, till her fingers started to twitch like she was playing the piano. Across the landing, Davey mumbled in a dream. Her brothers and sisters were the map of her own land, their funny ways and habits, the way Lily always put her left boot on first and Len would pull at his earlobes when he was thinking and Tom cracked his knuckles finger by finger. Same as how she knew Mam from the inside out, which is how she was certain the telegram had brought trouble, even though Mam had slipped it into her apron pocket without saying a word. May still hoped it might have been from Aunt Emma or Lily, but she'd seen how Mam's eyes had sunk deeper into her face and ever since she'd found it hard to breathe.

Crossing the bedroom floor, careful to miss the creaky boards, she lifted the doorlatch and slipped out onto the landing. She cocked her head to listen for a change in Davey's breathing, but it stayed deep and rhythmic, and she was about to start down the stairs when she noticed Mam sitting at the kitchen table, her face in her hands, shoulders slumped. As May hesitated on the landing, she heard a tap at the kitchen window and saw Mam's head go up like a pointer. She let out a stifled cry and ran out of sight. The door dragged on the flagstones as always, then there was silence except for little gasps and whispers and throat clearings. She saw her mother being half carried into the kitchen in the arms of a man in uniform who eased her down into the chair. The man took off his cap and laid it on the table beside the pot. Even with his hair shaved almost to the nub, May saw it was Tom and knew at once that Len must be dead.

Something scooped the breath from her belly and left her suspended. Then the sorrow swept in like she'd swallowed something so hot it burned her insides raw. She slid to the floor of the landing and pulled her knees to her face, staring and staring into the close dark cave of her arms. Len gone, taken away. How could it be? Len, gentle, kindly Len, with his reddened cheeks, pale eyes, and thin wrists. She raised her head and looked down on Mam and Tom, hoping she'd been wrong, but they were crying together, hands clasped on the table, Mam's head on her outstretched arms.

Tom's face was grey and unshaven, and May could smell him even from the landing, the sweet reek of rot. He pulled his hands gently away from Mam's and lit a cigarette from the lamp, putting the funnel back with badly shaking hands. "You can't blame him for running away, Mam, no one could. It was more terrible than you can imagine."

The catch in his voice made May's chest fold inwards. She bit her knuckles not to cry out. Tom reached into his tunic pocket and held out an envelope. "He wrote this to you before… while he was waiting for them to take him away."

Mam bent her chin towards her chest and May saw her shoulders rise. "I can't. You read it, son."

He put the letter on the table and looked at it as he dragged at his cigarette. Mam handed him a knife, and he broke the seal and unfolded the two sheets of squared French paper. "See, no censor marks. Because I brought it myself."

Mam turned her head away from the writing like it could burn her eyes.

"All right," Tom said, drawing again on his cigarette, then balancing it on the rim of a saucer. He pressed the letter to the table with the palms of his hands, cleared his throat and began to read in a strangely sing-song voice.

Dear Mam,

It seems I've done wrong. Everyone is angry with me. I ran off, Mam – I couldn't help it. I never thought they'd miss a nobody like me. I'm ashamed. I knew it wasn't right but I was so afraid.

When I joined up, I didn't know it would be like this. I didn't have any idea. It's like the worst nightmare you can think of but worse."

"He's right about that," Tom said.

The waiting was what did me in, Mam. We stood to at dawn, waiting by the firestep waiting to go over, bayonets fixed and vicious sharp. We'd had our rum ration and it made me feel warm all the way through and like I could do anything. But then they made us stay there for hours and hours, and I got more and more cold and more scared. And when at last we did go over, all that nice rum courage was gone. We set off running and shouting up that slope towards all the barbed wire. At first there was no firing and then all of a sudden it started with a terrific roar and men fell down like they were being scythed. I saw George Coulter hit and the blood came out of his throat like a waterspout. He fell back and landed funny. I was lying flat on my belly holding onto tufts of grass and men were running over me and swearing at me to get a move on. I crawled behind George - I even turned him on his side to make a bigger shield, so I could half crawl underneath him. You mustn't tell his mam. I felt him jerk as he was hit again and I could smell burning and his blood was all over me, dripping in my eyes. The noise was so loud I couldn't think. The shells seemed to be coming from everywhere – not just from the front but from behind as well. Someone tripped over me and swore and then he choked and fell right next to me. His chest was ripped open. I could see his mashed-up insides all red and wet and full of bits of bone, and the worst of it was he was looking right at me, Mam, his eyes were wide open and he wasn't dead.

The sing-song was gone; Tom's voice was unsteady. May felt sick and dizzy and made herself breathe through her nose.

I lay there for hours. I was shaking like a dog, Mam, and crying. The sky got dark and the firing mostly stopped. I knew they'd come looking for the wounded so I couldn't stay where I was, so I ran and ran. I hid in a ditch for a while, but it was cold and wet so I pressed on. That's when I found a dry place in a funny kind of old mine tower, and I must have fallen asleep because next thing I knew some MPs were shouting and dragging me up from the floor.

They're going to shoot me in the morning. I know I deserve it but I'm so afraid, Mam. I'm praying God will forgive me for my weakness and won't send me to the eternal fire, though honestly I don't know if it could be any worse than that hill yesterday. Surely when someone tries to kill you again and again, it must be right to try to save yourself.

Please forgive your poor weak son, Mam, and think of me kindly sometimes. Kiss the girls and Davey for me. Tom will see you all right. Love from your Len xxx.

May sobbed into her fists, clenching every muscle to hold back the noise of it. It bent her in two to think of his terror, his crumpled bleeding body. Len, sweet Len, who'd lift her up to stroke the horses' noses, who'd walk with her past the churchyard at dusk when she was afraid of the dead people in the ground. The brother who always waited for her to catch up and never made her feel like the baby. It bubbled up from her core, the longing to see him and the terrible fact that she never ever would again. Like she'd never see Dada again either, left with only the dusty rack of pipes beside his chair and the worn spot in the rug made by his feet.

Mam was crying into her folded arms on the table, saying Len's name over and over. Tom tipped out another cigarette from his pack, and with shaking hands, lit it from the first, then crushed the tiny stub in the saucer. Smoke drifted up the stairs towards

May, and she breathed it in. Mam lifted her head. "Were you with him?"

"They locked me up, so I wouldn't cause a fuss. But I saw him… after."

"Was he peaceful?"

May saw Tom bend his head as if the memory were a heavy weight around his neck. "Oh Mam, he looked so young. Almost the way Davey would look if he weren't… how he is."

Davey. He would have to hear the news. He would rage and howl and weep, and they'd have to hold him down and stroke and console him till the worst was over. May wiped her nose and eyes on the hem of her nightgown. She was going to have to be strong for him and for Mam, that was all.

"What about you, son? Have you been going on alright? You look so dirty. Is this how the army takes care of its men?"

"I'm sorry, Mam, there was no time to bathe. I only have a week's pass, and it took me two days to get here. The train from London was full of wounded officers. I didn't know the Hall had been requisitioned."

"I must have told you."

"We don't always get to read letters through before something happens. Oh, but the CO's a good bloke – he's related to the family at the Hall. A nephew or something. Captain Crowindale. He has a title, but he doesn't come it with us enlisted men. He's the one who gave me leave to bring Len's letter to you."

"Didn't stop him from having our boy shot though."

"I think he tried, Mam. It was Brigade, they wanted Len made an example of. He tried to tell them Len was ill, but no one would listen."

Mam leaned her head on her folded hands, then stood up, suddenly, opened the range door and threw in a log. "Let's get you washed, son. I don't want your sisters and Davey seeing you like this in the morning. It's going to be hard enough for them hearing the news."

Tom shook his head slowly, looking down at his black finger-nails. "It's bad, Mam. There's lice everywhere."

Mam paused, wiping her hands on her apron. "Is that why you shaved off your hair?"

"I couldn't bear the itching."

She put both hands on the table and looked him in the face. "Then let's get those things off you and make you clean and tidy. Now you go and fill this kettle good and full, and I'll bring in the copper and the bathtub."

Tom pushed back his chair, the cigarette dangling from his mouth, and both he and Mam moved out of May's sight.

She wrapped her arms around herself, wishing she'd brought a shawl from the bedroom, wishing she could creep down and sit by the fire, but it would be as bad as interrupting a sermon and she knew she'd hear more truth if they didn't know she was listening. So, she held her cold-numbed feet in her hands and watched in the mirror over the mantelpiece as Tom took off his uniform, piece by piece. First, the tunic was dropped into the copper, then Tom unlaced his boots, unwound his puttees, slid down the braces and unbuttoned his trousers. If he'd looked up into the mirror, his eyes might have met May's where she sat in the deep shadow in the turn of the stair, but he was bound up in the circle of light from the lamp, absorbed in his task. The grey flannel shirt with the number on a white strip across his belly, his vest and long johns all came off and into the copper, and May could see the dirty line around his neck and the bumpy red bites on his long white back.

Mam shuddered. "I see the lice in the seams, the horrible things."

Tom stood shivering on the rug in his underpants, stubbing out his cigarette. May heard Mam take the copper with the filthy uniform out to the yard. She hurried back to lift the kettle before it began to whistle and carefully poured the boiling water into the tub, which May knew would already hold an inch or two of water from the pump so it wouldn't scald. "Let me boil up another kettle, son, make it nice and full," Mam said, but Tom held out his hand to stop her. "You needn't trouble. This'll be grand."

As he untied his pants and eased himself into the steaming tub, May turned away so she wouldn't see the floppy thing between his legs. He let out a groan.

"I'm sorry, son, but it has to be good and hot to kill those lice eggs."

"It's a'right, Mam, it feels good," he said, settling back, his eyes closing.

Mam rubbed the carbolic soap between her hands. "May I wash your poor head?"

Eyes closed, Tom nodded, his reddened arms lying along the edges of the tub. Mam put her soapy hands on his scalp, white with patches of peppery stubble, and pressed her fingers into the skin, rubbing the seam of his skull, the cords of his neck, his temples. Tears rolled down his face. "I can't go back, Mam, I can't."

Mam touched his face, leaving a trail of lather to his chin. "Oh son, I wish with all my heart you didn't have to."

"I could bear it when I was with the horses. It's mostly behind the lines and it's something I could do. The Captain tried to get Len and me transferred back to Transport, but bloody Brigade wouldn't have it."

Mam shook her head. "The things Len said in his letter, about the fighting – there's been nothing about it in the papers."

Tom moved his legs, slopping water onto Mam's apron. "If they told you at home what it's like, no one would stand for it. You know what I can't stop thinking about? Lying wounded in a shell hole, knowing you're a goner, not able to move a muscle. The rats'll eat the eyes out of a man's face – a wounded man, Mam. A man who's still alive."

Mam brought her arm up to her face, and May couldn't tell if it was to wipe away sweat or to ward off his words. "No, son, it can't be. Those are just tales they tell to frighten you. I'm sure they rescue the wounded straight away."

Tom shook his head. His eyes were open wide now, fixed on a point near Dada's chair. "You've never seen such big rats, Mam. They live inside the corpses, eat them from the inside out. The dead are everywhere – you can't help stepping on them. They let out the most awful smell."

Mam made a noise and jerked her head away, but Tom kept talking. "You can't help but touch them – on fire steps, between duckboards. Bits of bone and even skulls with teeth in the trench walls. It gives you a turn."

Mam's face was a blue-white with slashes of shadow across each cheek. "You mean, they don't get a Christian burial? The Army leaves them there?"

"There're too many of them."

"What about our Len? Where is he? What happened to him?" Mam asked, and May heard the panic in her voice.

Tom wiped his face with his open palm, blinking the water out of his eyes. "The Captain told me he'd do right by him. I'm sure he and the Padre had him buried somewhere behind the lines."

"Thank God."

Mam rested her wet arms on the side of the tub, slumped with relief, but Tom still stared ahead like he was somewhere else. "You know the thing I'm most afraid of, Mam? Shall I tell you?"

May saw Mam's face, how she didn't want to hear another word, but had to stay as she was, kneeling and listening.

"I saw a man drown in the mud. You're supposed to hold onto the pack of the man in front so's not to slip off the duck-boards, but he let go and fell in. His pack was so heavy it dragged him down, and that mud's deep, Mam. It's like a bog or quicksand. Full of rot and dead horses and gas and rusty shrapnel that'll slice your arm off. And it pulled him down in inch by inch. He knew what was coming and he hadn't a chance. I saw his eyes, Mam, the whites all around like he couldn't believe it was going to happen. Then he screamed, Mam, and screamed and screamed." Tom's hands came up out of the water like he was pushing something away. "It took him five minutes to go under. Last thing he saw was our faces, just standing there gawping."

Mam's voice didn't even sound like her. "Nobody tried to help him?"

"The CO and the sergeant tried reaching him with some duck-boards, but the boards just sank in too. No one could help. And he's still in there. In the spring when things dry up, he'll still be there. That's how they find them, their eyes wide open."

Mam dropped the carbolic soap in the tub and got to her feet so quickly she had to put out a hand to the dresser to steady herself. "Wash yourself. Everywhere. Inside your ears and down below. I'll get you some of Dada's clothes. I'm going to burn that uniform."

Startled, Tom looked up at her. "But Mam, you can't."

"You won't be needing it."

Up on the landing, May held her breath.

"You're staying here."

"But Mam –"

"Wash!" she said, with the voice she'd used with them all as they grew, when she would brook no argument. In the mirror, May saw Mam bend to open a dresser drawer and bring out care-fully folded clothes that May recognised as Dada's. Corduroy trousers, a faded blue shirt, a woollen sweater knitted by Aunt Emma. May longed to press her face against them and breathe in the last trace of her father. She already knew the restless ache of wanting someone who was gone forever. An ache that rubbed like a new boot on a raw heel. New skin would grow over it in time, but the soft place was always there underneath. And now Len was gone too, a new wound broken open.

In the tub, Tom soaped and rinsed, and again May turned her head away as he stood up, naked and dripping, and rubbed himself down with a towel. Mam brought him Dada's clothes, and as he dressed, May rested her head on her knees and slid briefly into sleep. When she woke with a start, Tom and Mam were drinking tea at the kitchen table, and Tom had lit another cigarette. "You know, the CO said a funny thing to me when he dismissed me. He said, 'Don't come back.'"

"There you are. He sounds like a good man, your Captain."

"But how?"

Mam settled the cosy on the teapot. "If you got injured, you'd be discharged, right?"

"A Blighty?"

Mam shook her head. "What does that mean?"

"That's what the boys pray for – a wound bad enough to get sent home for the rest of the war."

Mam tapped the teaspoon against the edge of her cup. "Exactly."

Tom shifted in his chair. "But how? I'm a long way from the Front."

Mam pushed back her chair and vanished into the scullery. Tom tapped the cigarette against his saucer, carving off the long grey ash, and rubbed one hand over his stubbly head. May heard Mam's footsteps coming back and saw Tom's eyes widen. She was carrying a billhook, one hand round the wooden handle, the wide curving blade on the palm of the other.

May crushed her fists against her mouth.

"We'll say you were helping me cut back the hedge and your hand slipped."

Mam laid it down on the table, the blade yellow in the lamp-light. Tom looked up at her.

"You don't mean …?"

Mam stood over him, saying nothing. Tom groaned. "Can't I just run off somewhere far away? Ireland maybe?"

"That'll not alter things," Mam said. "They'd find you and shoot you like they did your brother."

He groaned again and held his head in his hands, his cigarette dropping ash on the table. "I can't do it, Mam. I haven't the guts."

"Then I'll do it."

"Oh!" May had said it out loud. She bit her knuckles and held her breath, afraid they'd heard, but they showed no sign. Mam sat down at the table. "Look at me, son. It's the only answer, you know it is. It has to be more than a nick – it has to lame you enough so you're no use to the Army."

"I'd have a crippled leg forever, is that the size of it?"

There was anger in his voice, but also fear. Mam took his hand in both of hers. "Tom. We can't lose you as well."

Something in her tone made him pause. "Has it been a struggle? You never said."

"Never mind that now."

Tom banged on his forehead with his fist, over and over. "I brought this on you, me and my stupid bluster. Len would still be alive if only we'd stayed at the farm. It's my fault."

Mam caught his fist and held it still. "No, son. I'm proud of you – both of you. You wanted to defend your country. It's the Army's fault. *They* shot Len, not the Germans. They don't deserve your loyalty."

They sat together, not moving, Tom's head bowed over his cup, his fist still in Mam's hands. A dusky light seeped under the curtains and into the corners of the kitchen, and May realised she'd been hearing the birds stirring for some time. Tom looked up. "Do you have anything strong in the house?"

"I've a bit of brandy."

Mam went to the pantry and came back with a bottle May had never seen. Tom poured the dark liquid into his empty teacup and threw it back in one deep swallow. Putting the cup down, he shuddered as he looked at the billhook. "Where will you do it? I mean, what part of me?"

Mam looked him over, and May could see her fighting to hold herself together. "Above the knee. There's more flesh there than the shin. Now don't you think about it, son. You're a strong young man, and you'll be alright."

She went to the window and drew back the curtain. "It's almost light enough now. We'll say we wanted to get an early start on that hedge. Are you ready?"

May saw Tom close his eyes, take a deep breath and pick up

the blade. As the door creaked shut behind them, May hunched herself close and small, feeling the loud throb of her heartbeat in her eyes and ears. Len was dead and Mam was going to take the billhook and slice Tom's thigh like suet. She felt the bile rise and almost retched but swallowed it down and down. So much horror to bear, so much to think about over and over till her brain felt like a million birds in a tiny cage, flapping and trampling for space, for escape. When she heard the scream, it sounded like Mrs. Coulter's pig being slaughtered – not a human noise – but then there was the thump of Davey's feet on the floor, and she stumbled half upright, legs frozen from sitting too long, and caught him by the knees as he burst out of the boys' room, his hands flat against his ears. As Ada's frightened face appeared in the doorway, May held on tight to her brother's legs and said over and over "It's all right. Mam's making it right. She's going to make it all come right."

End of Part Two

The story of Celia Mapperley, May Hallam, and their families continues and concludes in Part Three of *Ancestral Virgins*. Available to buy at all major retailers in both paperback and ebook.

REQUEST FOR REVIEWS
OF ANCESTRAL VIRGINS

"The Crystal Gazer" Gertrude Käsebier, 1904, printed 1910
Courtesy of National Gallery of Art, Washington, D.C. under
Creative Commons Zero (CC0)

If you've enjoyed reading *Ancestral Virgins*, please consider leaving a review on your favourite retailer's website.

To stay up to date on future publication news, I invite you to check out my website www.fionajmackintosh.com and subscribe to my blog and mailing list on substack.com/@fionamackintosh1.

ACKNOWLEDGEMENTS

They say that writing fiction is a solitary pursuit, but in my experience that's only partly true. The author must first get the story down on the page, but after that, it takes a village to perfect it and get it into the hands of readers. So this is a great big thank you from me to everyone who has helped me to get *Ancestral Virgins* out into the world.

I could not have told the stories of Celia Mapperley and May Hallam without the input of my wonderful beta readers Keith and Melanie Donohue, Jan Linley, Melissa Mackintosh, Beth Millemann, and Sibbie O'Sullivan. They kindly agreed to read my hefty manuscript and gave me detailed and thoughtful feedback, which made the novel better in many different ways. I'm also grateful to the members of my various writing groups over the years for their insights into earlier incarnations of the book.

I'd like to express my deep gratitude to my talented niece Florence Clementine for the cover designs of all three volumes of *Ancestral Virgins* and for her patience with my many requests and changes of tack. My profound thanks also go to Britta Jensen of The Writing Consultancy for copy editing the manuscript and doing the layout of the book and for a whole lot of handholding as I learned the self-publishing ropes! My appreciation is also very much due to Athena Pajer for doing a careful sensitivity read of the sections dealing with Davey Hallam.

Finally, my love and thanks go to my brother, Andrew Mackintosh, my webmaster extraordinaire, and to my husband

Michael Hook for his unconditional support and for never losing patience with my lifelong compulsion to make up stories.

ABOUT THE AUTHOR

Author photograph by D.J. Corey

Fiona J. Mackintosh lives in the suburbs of Washington D.C. with her husband. Born in New Jersey, she grew up in Scotland by the North Sea and worked in London for several years before moving back to the US. An ex-journalist, she is now a freelance editor.

Her short stories have been widely published on both sides of the Atlantic, and she is a past winner of the Fish Flash Fiction Award, the Bath Flash Fiction Award, and the Reflex Fiction Prize. She is also a proud recipient of an Individual Artist's Award in Fiction from the State of Maryland.

Her flash collection *The Yet Unknowing World* was published by Ad Hoc Fiction in 2021. *Ancestral Virgins* is her first published novel.

Read more of Fiona's work at www.fionajmackintosh.com.

 substack.com/@fionamackintosh1

9 789899 348231 6